MONTANA
GHOST STORIES

MONTANA GHOST STORIES

Eerie True Tales

Debra D. Munn

RIVERBEND
PUBLISHING

The stories in this book were originally published in *Big Sky Ghosts,* Volumes One and Two (1993, 1994), by Debra D. Munn

Published by Riverbend Publishing, Helena, Montana.

Printed in the United States.

1 2 3 4 5 6 7 8 9 0 MG 12 11 10 09 08 07

ISBN 13: 978-1-931832-76-2
ISBN 10: 1-931832-76-5

Riverbend Publishing
P.O. Box 5833
Helena, MT 59604
Toll-free: 1-866-787-2363
www.riverbendpublishing.com

CONTENTS

Things That Go Bump in Bannack

If having more than its fair share of shoot-'em-ups and hangings is what causes a place to be haunted, then Bannack, first capital of the newly created Montana Territory, should be fairly crawling with spooks. This typical Wild West gold mining town was, after all, the headquarters for outlaw sheriff Henry Plummer and his robber gang, the Road Agents, and it was also the place where many of them, including Plummer himself, were rounded up by a secret group called the Vigilantes and brought to justice on the gallows.

With so much robbing and killing in Bannack's past, we might reasonably expect to hear that Plummer's spirit takes occasional midnight strolls up Hangman's Gulch or that the shades of gunfighters frequently reenact their battles to the death inside Skinner's Saloon. Well, perhaps they do; though, to my knowledge, no one has seen them. For, oddly enough, in this real-life "ghost town" that knew so much well-publicized violence, almost all of it by men upon other men, the only ghosts I've been able to dig up have been those of women, children, and animals.

Lee Graves, a descendant of one of Bannack's founding families and himself a photographer and author of the delightful *Bannack: Cradle of Montana* (Helena, Mont.: American & World Geographic Publishing, 1991), admits that in a ghost town, tourists often come looking for spooky stories and if they don't actually find them, they imagine them.

"But there are a couple of tales that really do seem to have something to them," Lee said. "Several times, visitors have reported hearing a baby crying on the southeast side of town, in one of the old cabins that used to belong to early resident Amede Bessette. People ask whether anyone with small kids could be living there now. Of course, no one does, but the story is that either eight or fourteen babies died there of various diseases, including colic, typhoid fever, and smallpox. Epidemics of all kinds were quite common in the old days and many of the graves in the cemetery are for children who died in the mid to late 1880s. There are also quite a few from around 1913."

The ghostly crying is mentioned in a Halloween 1989 article by John Barrows of the Dillon Tribune. In "The Ghosts of Bannack," Barrows wonders whether the babies are still crying in memory of that long-ago sickness and death. Perhaps a more likely explanation for the eerie sounds, if they really exist, is that the babies' suffering was of such intensity that it somehow psychically imprinted the noise of their crying onto the walls or floors of the old cabin, to be "played back" under the right conditions.

A more classic Bannack ghost story involves Lee Graves' godmother Bertie Mathews who died several years ago at the age of ninety-three. "When she was a young girl, her best friend was a gal named Dorothy Dunn, and those two kids were as close as they could be," Lee explained. "One summer day Bertie and Dorothy were together in one of those big swimming holes in Grasshopper Creek. I don't recall how it happened, but somehow, Dorothy drowned. Her death really bothered Bertie and she went through many hard times because of it.

"Sometime later, when Bertie was in her mid-teens, she was walking in the upper story of the old Meade Hotel, which her mother managed at various times through the years. Suddenly, she saw an apparition of her beloved friend. Dorothy was wearing a long blue gown, and her hair was flowing.

"This incident scared Bertie so much that she hardly ever talked about it," Lee said. "When I was a kid, my dad and I used to visit her quite often and, although he repeatedly asked her to tell us the ghost story from the hotel, she always refused. She would try to laugh it off and change the subject. But her older sister Georgia finally told Dad what Bertie had seen. All I know is that if Bertie said it happened, it did. She wasn't superstitious at all, and she was quite religious."

Other stories about the Meade Hotel involve dogs that refuse to go inside. One of these dogs belonged to Dr. Dale Tash, the present curator of Bannack and professor of history at Western Montana College at Dillon. While Dr. Tash firmly rejects the idea that phantoms exist, at Bannack or anywhere else, he did admit that his dog was frightened, and of an entity much more horrifying than a mere specter—a skunk!

If they are indeed true, two final legends about Bannack appear to have all the right ingredients for ghost stories, but strangely enough, I found none in connection with them. In spook lore from around the world, one of the surest ways to stir up spirits is to bury someone improperly or to disturb that person's final resting place. When Henry Plummer and two of his Road Agents were hanged in the wintertime, on January 10, 1864, the ground was frozen hard and the gravediggers didn't feel like going out of their way to bury what they regarded as lowlife scum. Therefore, the bodies of Plummer and the two men hanged with him, as well as that of another Road Agent hanged previously, were all buried fairly close to the surface.

According to Lee Graves, a few years afterward a doctor who was interested in Plummer got very drunk one night and dug up one of the outlaw's arms. "No one is sure who the grave robber was, but he may have been Dr. Glick, the same physician who had taken care of Plummer years before when he'd been shot in the elbow," Lee explained. "But whoever the man was, he was extremely inebriated and because he was on his way to a dance he thought he'd better get rid of his grisly find. So he left Plummer's arm, still covered with flesh, in a snowbank outside the dance hall.

"The doctor then went inside to enjoy himself, but he got a big surprise about thirty minutes later. His dog had been digging around in the snowbank, latched onto Plummer's arm, and carried it right into the dance hall to savor it in warmth and comfort. You can imagine how fast that broke up the party."

In his book on Bannack, Lee Graves tells two versions of another local legend about the fate of Henry Plummer's remains. The first and most probable says that around the turn of the century two drunks dug up Plummer's skull and deposited it on the back bar of Bannack's Bank Exchange Saloon. There the curious relic reposed until the saloon burned and, with it, all its contents. The second story is undoubtedly just that, a story, but is nevertheless fascinating. This account relates that the same old drunks dug up the skull, which finally found its way into the hands of a Bannack doctor. The unnamed doctor sent the specimen "back east to a scientific institution for study to try to figure out why Plummer was so evil."

If this second version has any truth at all, no one knows just what conclusions were supposedly drawn about Henry Plummer's nasty character. But it does seem a bit odd that Bannack isn't swarming with the ghosts of Plummer and his Road Agents. Could it be that they had enough of terrorizing their fellow citizens while they were alive?

If the outlaws ever do decide to return, they will still be able to recognize their old stomping grounds. True, over the years fires have taken their toll on some buildings, others have simply deteriorated and fallen down, and some structures have been moved (in the case of the Goodrich Hotel, all the way to Virginia City, about eighty-five miles away). Other buildings were torn down for their lumber or even for firewood, but Plummer-era landmarks such as the Crisman Store, the Carrhart House, and the Xavier Renois House are still standing. It is the goal of the Montana Department of Fish, Wildlife and Parks to preserve rather than to restore Bannack, so that this little mining town will never be the flashy, overly commercialized tourist trap that some other historical places have become. Instead, Bannack will always be a ghost town in the truest sense of the word.

THE GHOST WHO DIDN'T LIKE THE ROLLING STONES

(AND OTHER SPOOKS AT THE UNIVERSITY OF MONTANA)

MISSOULA

Most hauntings take place in a fairly limited locale—a particular room, a specific hallway, or a certain floor of a multistoried structure. But the University of Montana in Missoula has no fewer than four haunted buildings and the spooks inside don't restrict their supernatural shenanigans to any special areas—they seem to enjoy wreaking havoc throughout.

Take the old theater in the Fine Arts building, for example. Here a spiteful phantom plays tricks on people such as Mary Vollmer Morrow, a student at the university from 1973 to 1977. Years later, Mary still gets the creeps when she thinks of the time she was teased by the ghost.

"A group of us were leaving for a Montana Repertory Theater tour and we were supposed to meet early in the morning at the Fine Arts building," she explained. "I arrived before anyone else, around five o'clock, and even though I hated being alone in that place, I went inside. I kept wishing the others would show up and, finally, I heard the outside door open. Then I felt a draft, just as if someone had come in.

"Glad that somebody was there to keep me company, I ran to see who it was. But when I got to the door, I found it still locked with no sign that anyone had come through it. I stood there puzzled, and I heard the opening and shutting of the other door where I had just been waiting and felt another draft. I ran back again, but no one was there either, and that door was still locked too. This sequence of events happened four or five times, making me so uncomfortable that I decided to wait outside."

Mary also recalls that faculty members often brought their children to rehearsals and on more than one occasion the kids looked down from the balcony where they were playing and saw a mysterious person sitting in the audience. "None of us on stage could see him, but the children insisted he was there," she said.

The strangest occurrences from Mary's days at the university came during a production of Macbeth, always considered the "unlucky" play by theater folk. "The night of the dress rehearsal, the entire set, including a specially built staircase, collapsed," she remembered. "And on opening night, during the scene when Duncan and his army come in, our fog machine wouldn't turn off, so the entire auditorium filled with fog. The actors couldn't see the set or each other and kept falling off the stage and the audience couldn't see the actors.

"I played one of the three witches in that play, and as we stood over our boiling cauldrons and called out names of demons, we heard horrible screams coming from the back of the theater. We asked other people about them later, but apparently no one else had heard them. I don't know whether or not the ghost was responsible for all these things, but we found out firsthand that Macbeth really is the unlucky play."

Mary added that no one knew for sure whose spirit was haunting the theater, but most people believed it to be that of a worker reportedly killed during construction of the building.

Whoever the entity may be, other people have also reported feeling his presence. The drama department's production coordinator, Steve Wing, felt an eerie sensation in one of the hallways of the old Fine Arts building. "I was working alone late one night in 1977 or 1978," he explained. "My office is up on the second floor and I was leaving it to go down to the theater. As I walked into this one narrow hallway with a door at each end, I just sensed that someone was there with me. I can't explain it any better than that, but the feeling was so oppressive that I put on my coat and left."

Brantly Hall is another haunted building on the University of Montana campus and the ghost there is supposed to be that of a student who committed suicide. Rumors such as this one are often hard to verify and different versions of the suicide story exist. One is that the student killed herself in the basement, while another is that she threw herself out a window. The most bizarre version of all is the one that former student Stacey Gordon heard, that the suicide victim was a young woman who stabbed herself with a metal comb after her father lost money in the stock market crash of 1929. "I went to the university for a year," Stacey said, "and I remember hearing that her dog, a German shepherd, was also supposed to be haunting Brantly Hall."

No one I talked to reported any phantom dogs, but custodian Daniel Boone has definitely experienced eerie feelings in the old hall. "Rumor has it that the student who killed herself lived on the second floor when Brantly was still a dorm," he explained. "It was later turned into an administrative office building and, because of the extensive remodeling, it's now hard to pinpoint where the suicide was supposed to have occurred."

"I used to be a custodial crew chief in that building and I got chills every time I walked down the hallway," Daniel admitted. "One time in 1987 another guy and I were alone in Brantly Hall when it was all locked up. As we were walking through the building, we both got the same tingling up and down our spines and, on the third floor, we kept hearing a noise like someone clapping his hands together. The sound seemed to be coming out of the ceiling and it was very loud.

"We finished making the rounds of the third floor and when we came back to the stairwell where we had been earlier, a yellow slicker raincoat was lying there. We knew it hadn't been there just a few minutes before and we were certain that we were the only people in the building. And, all the while, we kept hearing that loud, inexplicable clapping sound, which gave us a prickly feeling on the backs of our necks. The noise finally became so unbearable that we left and, ever since, I've been leery of going back."

Whether or not the suicide rumors at Brantly Hall have any basis in fact, they tend to make people nervous. Drama professor Rolly Meinholtz recalls the time that one of his students, a young man from Korea, was rehearsing for an outdoor theater production. In one scene, he seemed to be hanging himself from a tree outside Brantly Hall. Campus police became so alarmed at what they feared to be history repeating itself that they rushed to his aid. Needless to say, the student was stunned at having his rehearsal interrupted so dramatically.

Another haunted location on the University of Montana campus is Jeannette Rankin Hall, named for the state's first woman senator. This building began as the university's library, but later became the law school. Now it is used mainly for classrooms. Custodian Jack Mondloch has heard doors closing when he knew that no one else was in the building and his boss, Jeanne Tallmadge, had an even stranger experience in the summer of 1981.

"A large crew doing extra cleaning was on campus and another man and I were in charge of it," she said. "He and I got together each night in Rankin Hall to discuss the next day's work and at that time we also cleaned the top floor, which consists of four classrooms.

"Generally in the summertime the buildings are only lightly used, but on one particular night we heard the sound of subdued voices coming through the closed door of the northeast classroom. It sounded as if fifteen to twenty-five people were in there carrying on a conversation, but we couldn't distinguish any of the words.

"We figured it was a class or discussion group, so we kept waiting right outside the door for it to be over," Jeanne explained. "It got later and later and at eleven-fifteen I decided it was time for those people to get out.

"I opened the door to tell them to leave—and there was not a single soul in that room. Not one person. I ran to the windows and looked out, thinking that maybe the voices of people outside had carried so that they sounded as if they were in the classroom. But no one was there, either.

"I was completely baffled by this experience," Jeanne confessed, "but when I told other people about it, they claimed to have experienced the same thing."

Just a few nights after hearing the "phantom class," Jeanne had another weird experience involving Rankin Hall. "I was walking away from the building when something made me turn around and look back," she said. "All the lights were blazing in those second floor classrooms, even though I'd just turned them off. I went back upstairs and switched the lights off again, but by the time I got outside they had come back on. At that point, I decided they could just stay that way, because I was not going to enter that building again.

"The same thing happened over and over that summer and one night I was with another person on the second floor when the hall light began to dim as if it were being controlled by a dimmer switch. Finally, it went off completely. Electricians took the lights apart to check them, but they couldn't figure out why they went on and off like that.

"Nobody really knows who or what is haunting Rankin Hall," Jeanne explained, "but since it used to be the law building, we like to joke that the ghost is somebody who never got over failing the bar exam."

Fellow custodial worker Bob Williams has noticed that the odd phenomena in Rankin Hall tend to occur most frequently from August through October, during a full moon. Bob's first unusual experience there occurred one August night in 1984 or 1985. "I heard noises downstairs and decided to check them out," he told me. "As I went to go down the stairs, the light in the stairwell went off. I thought someone was playing around, so I went up the stairs and turned the light back on. I started to go back down and off it went again. I walked up and turned the light on one more time and I kept my eyes on the switch in the lower section to see who was playing a joke on me.

"As I was going down the stairwell, the light went off again, but I could tell that no one had flipped the switch. So I went back up and turned it on one more time and started down the stairs. Sure enough, the light went off again. This time I just kept walking and the light continued to turn itself on and off, on and off. I'd had enough, so I left to have a cigarette."

Bob explained that for a while he wondered whether a certain coworker hadn't somehow played a trick on him. "But then I found out that he had been way off in a different building at the time," he said. "Again, we had electricians check for wiring problems, but they found nothing that could explain the strange behavior of the lights."

Bob's eeriest occurrence at Rankin Hall took place on another late evening after the building had been locked up. "I was working in a little computer room off the main staircase when I heard a noise upstairs," he said. "I went to the second floor, but found nothing out of the ordinary except some chairs in disarray. I straightened them up and went back to the first floor to resume cleaning, when I clearly heard someone walking around upstairs. This time I stepped outside the building and hollered up at the second floor, but no one responded.

"I went back inside and I clearly heard footsteps coming down the stairs—but no one was there," Bob insisted. "I continued to hear them walking right in front of me and, as they did so, I felt a cool breeze and smelled a dank, musty odor. And then the footsteps went on into the basement. As you can imagine, I finished cleaning very quickly and got out."

Bob Williams has also encountered unexplained phenomena in University Hall, which contains administrative offices. Also referred to as Main Hall, this building has probably been the setting for more weird goings-on than any other on campus. "When we got ready to leave, we often heard doors slamming shut throughout the entire building," Bob remembered. "At first we thought a prankster was to blame, but it happened so often that people were becoming afraid to work there.

"One time we set a trap to catch the culprit," Bob continued. "We went through the building, shutting and locking all the doors, and we stationed people near all the exits. With everyone and everything ready, we waited and sure enough, the slamming started again.

"Several guys rushed to check the doors and what they found was startling. Some doors that we had locked were unlocked; some were open and some were closed and we didn't find anyone who could have interfered with them. The door slamming continued the whole time I worked nights, and it was most frequent between 11:00 P.M. and 1:00 A.M. It's probably still going on and nobody has ever been able to explain."

Daniel Boone has also heard the doors slam when he knew that no one else was in the building. "And these doors are solid wood, about two inches thick, with deadbolt locks on them," he explained. "Even air blowing through drafty windows wouldn't be enough to move doors that heavy. Lights also come on by themselves and we all joke about wanting to get the second and third floors cleaned before sundown, because nobody likes to be up there after dark. I'm a rational, sensible person, but I admit that several times I've been scared to death in Main Hall."

Daniel's fellow custodian Jack Mondloch said he never believed in ghosts before he started working at the university, but one night in Main Hall he heard phantom footsteps descending a staircase—while he happened to be standing at the bottom of it. Jack claims that he wasn't frightened, but merely surprised by this eerie encounter. However, another experience made him believe that the spooks were trying their best to intimidate him.

"One night I was cleaning the sinks in the men's room in the basement of Main Hall," he explained. "I was six or eight feet from the door and I heard someone knocking. I said, 'It's open,' but no one came in. I heard another knock, so I went over and opened the door myself and was surprised to find no one there. Now, this building has long, creaky, wooden hallways, and you can hear every move that anyone makes. And I opened up that door so fast that there was no time for any trickster to get away.

"I didn't want to put up with any more invisible people knocking at the door, so the next night I propped it open with a wedge," Jack said. "I was working at the other end of the bathroom, when—boom! The wedge came flying through the air and hit me in the leg. I looked all over the place for whoever had thrown it, but there was nobody anywhere near me. I felt irritated by this little episode—it was as if somebody were telling me, 'Take that!'"

Fellow custodian Jim Dredger laughed when he heard Jack's story, but one night he discovered for himself that Main Hall was haunted. "I was downstairs in the women's restroom around 1:00 A.M., filling up the soap dispensers, when I heard a knock at the door," Jim said. "I put the soap down and yelled, 'Come on in; I'll be out in two or three minutes.' There was no answer, and then I heard another knock. I walked over to the door, opened it up, and found no one there.

"I thought this was peculiar, but I figured that my supervisor or one of my friends was giving me a bad time, so I didn't think too much about it. But just to be on the safe side, I stuck a wedge under the door to keep it open. That way, if I heard someone walk by, I could look out and see who it was. I turned back around to pick up the soap canister and there in the mirror of the vanity was the reflection of a lady with dark hair.

"I was startled and I whirled around to see what she wanted, but there was no sign of her. I rushed into the hall, but I couldn't see or hear anyone moving along that wooden floor. I felt very strange, and I hesitated to tell anyone what had happened because I'd made so much fun of everyone else's ghost stories."

No one seems to have any idea who the entity haunting the building might be, but at least one custodian learned something about the phantom's taste in music.

"When I worked in Main Hall, I often took my Walkman stereo with external speakers," explained MaryJane West. "Normally, I used headphones, but the building was so creepy that I wanted to be able to hear what was going on around me. I played all kinds of music from country to experimental rock and I soon learned that every time I played the Rolling Stones or the Clash, the tape player would shut off. It didn't matter whether I was sitting right next to it or across the room—it would shut off whenever I played tapes of those two groups.

"The first few times I thought there was something wrong with the tapes. But when I played them at home, or even in buildings other than Main Hall, they worked fine. And even in Main Hall I could listen to them as long as I wore my headphones. I guess the ghost didn't mind my listening to the Stones or the Clash, as long as it wasn't subjected to them too."

The phantom music critic and the other unearthly beings at the University of Montana give new meaning to the term "school spirit," as they've certainly done their part to make campus life more interesting. With four haunted buildings and many reports of unexplained phenomena in each one, this university surely deserves a number-one ranking as a setting for the supernatural.

GHOSTS OF THE
LITTLE BIGHORN BATTLEFIELD

Without a doubt, the newly renamed Little Bighorn Battlefield National Monument, in Crow Agency about fifteen miles outside of Hardin, is the most famous haunted location not only in Montana but arguably in the entire western United States. Known previously as Custer Battlefield National Monument, the site has been the center of controversy and mystery ever since Lieutenant Colonel George Armstrong Custer led his ill-fated raid on a village of Lakota Sioux and Cheyenne on a hot Sunday afternoon in June 1876.

Custer and his Seventh Cavalry were part of the U.S. government's campaign to solve what it called the "Indian problem" once and for all. Three separate expeditions, led by George Crook, John Gibbon, and Alfred Terry, were to close in on so-called hostile Sioux who had refused to be herded onto the hated reservations. The plan was for Custer and his troops to march into the valley of the Little Bighorn River and to wait for battalions led by Terry and Gibbon to meet them on June 26.

The reasons why Custer did not wait for the backup troops are still debated. His supporters say that when scout reports told of a large encampment of Sioux, Custer simply wanted to keep the Indians in check before they could escape. He probably also feared that he and his forces had already been sighted by the enemy. Critics charge, however, that since the Democratic Convention was due to be held on June 27, Custer wanted to win a major battle against the Indians in time to be nominated as the presidential candidate. Whatever his reason for haste, on June 25 Custer decided to attack. He divided his forces into three groups, a move that was to prove disastrous.

Captain Frederick Benteen led his soldiers to scout for Indians to the southwest of the encampment, while Major Marcus Reno and his troops went to attack the southern end. Custer and more than two hundred of his men headed north of the Indian village and positioned themselves along the ridge.

When Reno's men began their raid on the unsuspecting village around 3:00 P.M., they were dismayed by the fierceness and strength of the Indians, who soon forced their attackers across the river and up into the hills. Almost a third of Reno's troops were dead or missing by the time the rest of them reached the bluffs.

Captain Benteen's forces reached Reno's around 4:15 P.M. and began organizing a defense. But by this time the Indians had already detected Custer's forces near the northern part of the encampment and some had turned their attention away from the counterattack on the southern end to focus attention on the soldiers on the ridge.

In fact, it was probably 3:45 P.M. when Sioux and Cheyenne warriors attacked Custer and his men, overwhelming them with greater numbers and more and better weapons than the Seventh Cavalry knew they had. The battle probably took only an hour or so and at the end Custer and all his men lay dead, many of them mutilated with axes, clubs, and arrows. Some of the wounded who were still conscious could do little but lie in wait as they heard the screams of fellow soldiers being tortured by warriors and even by the Indian women. Worse yet, the injured knew it was inevitable that they themselves would soon be finished off with the same brutal treatment.

When the Sioux and Cheyenne had routed, stripped naked, and dismembered Custer's forces, they returned to lay siege to Reno's and Benteen's men. This fight continued on into the following day and might have gone on longer if the Indians hadn't discovered that Terry's and Gibbon's reinforcements were finally on the way.

Many unanswered questions remain, but what is known is that the Battle of the Little Bighorn claimed approximately two hundred and sixty men from the Seventh Cavalry and an undetermined number of Indians, probably from thirty to one hundred. It is also known that the horrifying events of that June 1876 have so imprinted themselves upon the battlefield that well over a century later they are still causing a wide variety of psychic phenomena.

Even before the battle began, Custer's wife Elizabeth was said to have had a premonition that she would never see her beloved husband again. In a December 1986 National Geographic article titled "Ghosts on the Little Bighorn," Robert Paul Jordan says that Libbie's strong sense of impending doom increased as she watched her husband's regiment depart from Fort Lincoln in Dakota Territory. "For as the rising sun played on the mist," Jordan writes, "a mirage had taken form and translated some of the Seventh Cavalry into ghostly horsemen in the sky."

At the same time, Jordan explains, the revered Sioux leader and medicine man Sitting Bull had a vision of "soldiers falling into the Indian camp upside down."

After Libbie's worst fears and Sitting Bull's prophecy were realized and the Battle of the Little Bighorn passed into history, the Crow people, who were the traditional enemies of the Sioux and Cheyenne and whose reservation today surrounds the battlefield, were the first to sense the psychic reverberations from that bloody day. According to Bob Reece's "Visitors of Another Kind," a paper presented to the Boulder Country Corral of Westerners on October 4, 1990, the Crow believed that when the superintendent lowered the flag at the National Cemetery each evening, the spirits were allowed to arise and journey forth. When the flag was raised again the next morning, the souls of the dead returned to their graves. Reece points out that to this day many Crow will not go near the battlefield after dark.

And they certainly aren't the only ones to experience eerie sensations at the site. Reece says that stories of weird happenings told by tourists and employees apparently began in the 1950s. Reece quotes Robert Utley, chief park historian at the battlefield from 1947 to 1952, who insists that there "was no ghost business going on" during his tenure. It seems probable, however, that the phenomena were indeed occurring but were not as widely reported. As Reece points out, Charles Kuhlman, author of "Legend into History" and other works on western themes, was rumored to have visited Last Stand Hill during those years in hopes of contacting Custer's spirit and on at least one occasion to have succeeded. Robert Utley denied that this happened, both to Reece and to me, but the rumor remains.

Utley's successor, James F. Bowers, readily admits that something unsettling happened to him at the visitor center just a few days after he arrived. He mentions the experience in

"An Historian Looks at Custer," an article appearing in the November 1966 issue of The Denver Westerners Monthly Roundup (vol. 17, no. 10, 4-5):

When I went to Custer Battlefield National Monument to assume the position of Historian in 1952, accommodations were (and still are) scarce near the site, and as my family wouldn't arrive for several days, I set up a cot and hot plate in the basement of the museum building. Here are stored the hundreds of artifacts, collections, and other donations which have been presented to the government over the last 90 years. By living right in the museum for a few days, I would have at my fingertips the source material necessary to steep myself in the information necessary for my job. During the day I read, asked questions and answered questions, and in the evening I would fix a bite to eat and then gather some material and read until nearly midnight. On about my third night, there I am reading, alone in that big building, with "Custer" all around me, when I hear the front door unlock, open, and someone walk across the floor to the office. Reaching over my head, I opened the door and yelled, "I'm down here." No answer. In a few moments, I heard the footsteps move into the museum area, and once again I hollered that I was down below. The steps cease, but still no answer to my call. When the steps move a third time toward the back door which led to the battlefield and was never unlocked, that was enough for me. I jumped up, locked the door, moved my cot into the darkroom of the photography lab and locked both those doors. There I spent the night and I don't remember that I slept much, either. Later, when I got the nerve to tell my story to the superintendent, he didn't laugh or poke fun at my imagination, but rather left me with the impression that I wasn't the first to have heard General Custer checking the area before turning in for the night.

Bower adds that he regrets not having had the courage to walk up the stairs to confront whoever was there. If his late night visitor really was Custer, Bower suggests, the spirit might have told him what really happened at Last Stand Hill.

Many other employees have also reported strange experiences in the visitor center at the base of this famous hill, but the phenomena have not always involved the ghost of Custer. Stephen Waring from Stoke-on-Trent in England worked as a volunteer in 1984 and he recalls the day in July or August when his friend saw the apparition of Major Edward S. Luce, a man who served in the Seventh Cavalry and who knew some of the men who fought in the Battle of the Little Bighorn.

"My friend was working at the battlefield as an Indian interpreter and he came running upstairs, saying that he had seen a ghost in the visitor center projection room," Stephen remembered. "At first he thought the man he saw was one of the seasonal rangers, but he soon realized that the figure was wearing old-fashioned clothes. My friend looked visibly shaken, and I honestly believe he saw the ghost of Major Luce."

It's hardly surprising that the major would want to remain at the battlefield after death since, following his retirement from the Army, he and his wife Evelyn spent fifteen years publicizing the site and turning it into a tourist attraction.

Stephen Waring himself had some eerie experiences in the same building in the fall of 1984, but he never knew who, or what, was to blame. "Every now and then when I went for a nightly walk, I would return to find all the lights in the visitor center switched on," he explained, "even though a few hours before, I had switched them off. I would turn them off again before leaving, only to have them come on again before everyone arrived for work the next morning. I didn't even try to explain to my supervisor why the lights had been left on all night.

"On another occasion the burglar alarm switched itself on," he continued. "It was set by turning a key clockwise until a red light came on. Once the alarm was set, a one-minute delay allowed everyone to leave the building. After that time, anyone still inside the visitor center would activate the alarm.

"One evening in October or November, between six and seven o'clock, I was finishing some paperwork in the general office. I heard a click which sounded like a key being turned. I don't know why, but I automatically thought of the burglar alarm and, sure enough, it had been switched on. The key was fully turned and the red light was on.

"Anyone in this situation would suspect that someone was playing a practical joke, but I knew full well that everyone else had gone home and I was alone. I made a quick search of the building and then rushed home myself. From then on, I would never stay in the visitor center on my own."

Charles Mulhair was another employee who had a brush with the supernatural in the same building. In the summer of 1988, he worked at the battlefield as a seasonal interpreter and his wife Karol ran the cash register in the museum bookstore. "One day I had just gone down into the book storage room in the southwest corner of the basement," he explained. "I opened the door and turned on the light and, as I did that, I saw a figure with his or her back to me, about fifteen to twenty feet from the door. The person took a step to the left and disappeared down the third aisle and I wondered why anyone would have been down there in the dark.

"At first I figured it was probably my wife, although everything happened so fast that I couldn't even tell what sex the person was. I said something and walked over to where he or she had been, but I couldn't see anyone. I got a funny feeling and walked out of the room. I doubted myself for a while, but I still recall seeing what was definitely a human form. The person seemed to be wearing a sweater, so maybe that's why I thought it was a woman."

Other employees have reported being physically touched by an invisible phantom. In the summer of 1990, a volunteer was standing behind her desk when she felt someone gently place a hand on her shoulder. She turned around quickly, but no one was there and a check through the offices failed to turn up anyone. An even stranger occurrence the same year was reported by an assistant historian, who felt someone grab his leg when he was giving a program. He looked down and saw no one, but later that day on his way home he suddenly had the urge to veer off in a different direction. Obeying the impulse, he walked through part of the cemetery where he discovered an old cavalry bridle. Ever since, he has wondered whether the two events were in some way connected.

Maintenance men are in an especially likely position to experience odd phenomena at the visitor center since they are so often alone there at all hours of the day and night. Guy Leonard will never forget one early morning in July 1991 when he caught a glimpse of an apparition.

"It must have been about six o'clock, a good two hours before everyone usually comes in," he explained. "I was vacuuming, going from one office to the next, when out of the corner of my eye I saw a person standing about fifteen feet away from me. He was wearing a white, beige, or light brown shirt and he had a black or brown cartridge belt slung diagonally across his chest. I couldn't make out any facial features and he looked a little hazy. I wondered who could be in the building so early in the morning and, as I continued to look at him, he just faded away."

Guy says he wasn't frightened when he saw the phantom soldier, but he admits to having had a weird feeling on other occasions wher he heard doors opening and people walking when no one else was in the visitor center. "There's a small swinging door that says 'employees: only,'" he said. "Sometimes I hear that thing shut and when I go to see if anyone is there, the building is empty."

Guy was present on another occasion in the summer of 1991 wher a staff member heard a phantom voice from the theater downstairs. "We were getting ready to hold a CPR class in there," Guy recalled, "and one of the rangers asked this guy, 'Hey, Joe, are you going to take the CPR class again this year?' Joe answered, 'Yeah,' and went on downstairs to open up the back door leading into the theater. He and one of the medic out of Hardin were bringing in some gear for the class and when they both went in at one end of the room they heard a voice repeat, 'Hey, Joe, are you going to take that class this year?' Joe turned around to look, but could see no one. He asked the medic if he had spoken and the medic answered that he thought Joe had said something. Neither man had asked the question, but they both heard it. And they were sure that no one else was there.

"The creepy thing is that a tourist actually died of a heart attack right there in the theater two or three years ago," Guy explained. "So maybe his ghost wanted to make sure that Joe kept brushing up on his CPR techniques for the benefit of other people, even though it was too late to save him."

While a number of spooky things have taken place in the visitor center, even more have occurred in what is called the Stone House, built in 1894 as a residence for the superintendent of the National Cemetery. Now used to house summer staff at the battlefield, the two-story building is located beside the entrance gate to the vast graveyard, established in 1879, where among the thousands of dead are soldiers from other Indian battles and from conflicts as recent as the Vietnam War.

The oldest standing building in Big Horn County, the Stone House is considered by Bob Reece and others who have spent time there to be the center of supernatural activity at the Little Bighorn Battlefield. Perhaps this is only to be expected, since the basement of the structure was at one time used to store bodies before they were buried in the adjacent cemetery.

"Lights are frequently seen burning in different parts of the Stone House when the building is known to be empty," said Michael Moore, who began working as a living history interpreter in 1984. "During winter weather it's especially eerie when the lights come on, because often there are no tracks in the snow leading up to the place."

According to Bob Reece's paper, one former chief historian who lived on the battlefield during the winter reported that he often saw lights burning in the upstairs apartment of the Stone House. He always went to turn them off, but on one occasion he couldn't get the front door to open. Frustrated, he went home and returned an hour later, at which time the door opened easily.

Probably the strangest incident involving a light on in the Stone House occurred in 1980, on a mid-spring evening around sunset. Historian Mardell Plainfeather was returning to the battlefield after visiting some relatives when she noticed a light burning on the second story. She was well aware of the weird reputation of the Stone House, but since it was the time of year when housing for summer employees was being spruced up, she decided that the light probably had been left on by maintenance personnel.

Mardell stopped at the apartment of Mike and Ruth Massie, about two hundred yards below the Stone House, to ask Mike to go with her to turn off the light. Because Mardell had her small daughter with her, Mike volunteered to do the job himself.

"I went up the stairs of the old place and looked around to see if anyone was there," Mike recalled. "I couldn't see anybody, so I went on up to the second floor to flip the light switch off. As I started walking back to my apartment, my wife Ruth ran outside and I could see that she was shaken up.

"She had been watching television on a used set we had just bought in a repair shop in Hardin and, at the same time I was upstairs in the Stone House, a strange voice had suddenly spoken through the TV, saying only the words 'second floor.' Ruth knew that I was on the second floor of the Stone House and she wondered if everything was all right. We never could figure out why that eerie voice came out of the television, or what it meant."

Michael Moore was equally puzzled by some strange occurrences in the Stone House on a night in May 1989. "My roommate Michael Donahue and I had just finished a camp of instruction in Fort Laramie, Wyoming, and it was our first or second night back at the battlefield," he explained. "We were staying in the front room; a maintenance man sometimes stayed in the back room, but he wasn't there that night. I was still up reading and Mike had already fallen asleep.

"Between our room and the back room was a padlocked door. Suddenly I heard a noise as if someone were pushing on it and trying to get out. At first I thought I might have been imagining things, but then I heard it again a minute or so later. Mike was still asleep and I decided that the next time I heard the banging I'd wake him up to find out for sure whether anybody was staying in that back room.

"When the pounding began again, I tried to wake Mike to ask him, but he was so tired that he just mumbled something and went back to sleep. The sound came again two or three more times in the next five minutes and the last two bangs were really loud. I never did figure out what was causing this to happen—it wasn't even a windy night."

About sixteen months later, in September 1990, Michael Moore heard even stranger noises in the Stone House. "I was living there alone and I was up around midnight doing my laundry," he recalled. "The utility room was in a building about seventy-five yards away and I was carrying my clothes back home when I heard a noise like a door slamming somewhere inside the house.

"I thought that was odd since I was the only one living there, but I wondered whether a friend had dropped by to see me. I looked all over the house, but no one was there. I returned downstairs to fold my clothes and after about ten minutes I heard the sound of something heavy, such as a file cabinet, being turned over on either the second floor or up in the attic. This banging sound continued for an hour or two and I also heard what sounded like someone jumping off the couch upstairs and walking around. "There's a door at the top of the stairs and I could also hear its handle turning," Mike continued. "Just a day or so before I heard these things a maintenance man had been working on the roof and one of the chemicals he was using started a fire. The blaze was quickly extinguished, but I wondered whether it somehow triggered all the activity I heard upstairs." Regardless of the cause of the sounds, other people have also heard them. "Former staff member Joe Albertson and his wife Louise [not their real names] have spent many summers in the Stone House since the 1950s and they've heard and actually seen the door handle turning," Mike told me. "They've also heard the heavy thing being pushed over somewhere upstairs, as did a maintenance man in 1991. This guy also heard people screaming and children talking inside the building."

In addition to hearing mysterious noises inside the Stone House people have sighted apparitions there. Some have supposedly seen the ghost of Major Luce peering from the small round window at the top of the house and, according to Bob Reeve's paper, others have seen an unidentified woman's figure descending the stairs. Reece and Michae Moore were both told the story of a new battlefield ranger who was staying in an upstairs apartment of the Stone House. On his first night he awoke and felt someone sit down on the end of his bed. At first he thought the person was his wife, until he remembered that she was away, visiting her family. As the ranger reached for the Colt .45 lying on the nightstand, he was able to make out the shadowy form moving from the foot of his bed. As he continued to watch, he saw the torso of a soldier, minus the head and legs, move quickly across the room until it disappeared into an adjoining one.

The sighting of incomplete apparitions is not unusual, since it apparently takes an incredible amount of energy for one to appear at all: Ghost lore is replete with phantoms who look as if they have everything but a head, a right foot, or legs from the knees down, for example—and in most cases they appear this way not because their original physical bodies were similarly deficient, but because they lack enough energy for a complete materialization. In the case of apparitions at the Little Bighorn Battlefield, there may be another, albeit ghastly, reason why the do not appear entire.

When the forces of Terry and Gibbon arrived at the scene of the battle, they were sickened by the bloated and mutilated corpses of Custer troops. Custer's brother Thomas, for example, had been so horrible butchered that his body was identifiable only by a tattoo on his arm. Indian drawings depicting the slaughter also show clearly that the remains of many of the slain were beheaded and otherwise dismembered. An archeological examination of some of the skeletons proved that this kin of mutilation occurred. Is it not possible, then, that such horrific treatment of a body could cause its apparition to also appear in pieces?

But what caused the materialization of an Indian man in the bedroom on the top floor of the Stone House? Dan Martinez, now a historian at the Arizona Memorial Museum Association in Hawaii, still doesn't know what to make of an experience he had when he was a seasonal ranger and interpreter at the Little Bighorn Battlefield from 1979 to 1985.

"I admit that when I was a seasonal there, I used to make up scary stories about the Stone House so that other people would be afraid of it," he said. "That way, I could be sure of staying in the old place myself. I really enjoyed my time there and I never believed in such things as ghosts. But one night I experienced something I've never been able to explain. I don't know whether it was a dream or an actual occurrence, but if it was just a dream, it seemed terribly real.

"I think it was June 1982, and I remember waking up one night to find someone standing over me, right next to my side of the bed. It was a moonlit night and I saw without a doubt that this person was an Indian and he was just standing there and staring down at me.

"I was absolutely powerless to move or to wake my wife lying beside me. I couldn't even speak as I watched this man. At first I thought he was a real person, because he looked absolutely solid and was dressed in all the trappings of an American Indian. Most notable was an eagle feather hanging off to one side of his head. I could barely breathe and I felt as if there were a huge depression on my chest.

"My bed was against the wall and there was a doorway no more than three or four feet away. I still couldn't move, but my eyes rolled to watch as the man turned to walk out of the room. After he left, my heart was pounding and I was perspiring profusely, even though it was a cool night. I was just frozen with terror and it took me a while before I was able to wake up my wife.

"The whole experience lasted no more than a minute, but it seemed an eternity and had a profound effect on me, especially since I used to joke with others about their belief in the supernatural. To this day, the most disturbing thing about what happened is that I don't know whether it was a dream or reality."

Although the phantom in Dan Martinez's bedroom seemed menacing, at least one spirit in the Stone House has apparently acted in a benevolent way. Joe and Louise Albertson frequently experienced unexplainable occurrences during their many summers in the house, including footsteps from the empty upstairs and objects being mysteriously moved around. According to Bob Reece's paper, one day just as Louise was about to eat lunch, she heard a loud, high-pitched noise coming from the kitchen. It sounded like the whistle of a tea kettle, but no kettle was boiling at the time. Louise was just about to take her first bite when the whistle sounded louder. Perceiving that she was being warned about something, Louise looked at her lunch, which included some leftover chicken. She decided that it had spoiled and threw it away, feeling grateful to the spirit who might have saved her from food poisoning.

When Guy Leonard worked as a seasonal interpreter at the battlefield, he stayed for a while in the Stone House and never encountered anything out of the ordinary. But one day not long after he began working as a maintenance man in January 1991, he was sweeping and stacking boxes in the basement of the old house when he heard the sound of someone clearing his throat.

"My first thought was that my supervisor had come in and was trying to let me know he was there without startling me," Guy said. "I stopped and looked around, but no one was in the room; so I went over to the door that went upstairs. I checked everywhere and no one else was in the house. I even looked out the window and saw that there was only one set of footprints leading to the Stone House—and it was mine."

Not long afterward, on a night in March or April 1991, Guy's wife Janet was walking over by the Stone House to take a picture of the moon through the pine trees over the cemetery. As she lined up her shot to get the best picture, she heard someone say, "Hey, you there!"

Janet spun around, expecting to find a certain ranger who was staying at the battlefield during the spring season. She saw nobody, but she noticed lights on in the ranger's apartment a short distance away. She walked around the Stone House looking for the person who had spoken to her but she found no one. Thinking that perhaps a tourist might have parked a car by the main gates and walked in, she went to check, but there was no car and no sign of another person. Later, Janet learned that the ranger and his wife had been sitting in their living room watching TV at the time she heard the voice.

Employee living quarters other than the Stone House have also been the setting for psychic phenomena. Tim Bernardis, who came to the battlefield in 1983 as a participant in the Volunteer in the Parks program, lived in Apartment D, where he often awoke to see a figure standing at the foot of his bed. The sighting of "hypnagogic" images when one is in the stage between wakefulness and sleep is fairly common and is a little-understood function of the brain. Tim continues to see these "bedroom invaders" even away from the battlefield, but he had the experience most often while he was there.

"When I saw the figures, I'd shout, get up, and turn on the light," he said. "One roommate said I used to yell things like 'Get out of here' and 'What's going on?' But when I started leaving the door to my room open, I didn't see the images anymore—at least not while I was at the battlefield. I guess I felt safer with the door open."

Bob Reece was another participant in the Volunteer in the Parks program and he had an unusual experience one June night in the mid-1980s when he was staying with Doug Keller in Apartment A. "Douglas Ellison had also come to visit for a week or so," Bob recalled, "and early one morning, around three o'clock, I awoke to the sound of someone walking down the road from the direction of the Stone House. The person had a heavy step and was wearing boots. I assumed it was Ellison because he's a big guy over six feet tall and well built. The footsteps came closer and, just before they reached the apartment building, they stopped.

"By then I was wide awake. I listened for the sound of someone entering one of the other three apartments, which normally would have been impossible not to hear. No one went into any of them, however, and we found out later that Doug Ellison had ended up spending the night in Hardin. Doug Keller slept through the whole thing and I never heard the footsteps again after they stopped so abruptly."

A night or two later, Douglas Ellison heard the same mystery person strolling outside. "I had been out late with a local girl and when I returned to the apartment it was probably a little past midnight," he said. "The others were asleep until I came barging in, wide awake and talkative and, after five or ten minutes, they finally told me to shut up.

"I lay down on the floor in a comfortable spot and tried to sleep," Doug continued. "It must have been half an hour later when from outside I heard the sound of someone in heavy boots walking toward the apartment building. I figured it was just some guy coming home late as I had done; his heavy stride continued for perhaps seven or eight seconds, getting closer all the time. Then the walking just stopped.

"What gave me a start was that no lock turned, no door opened or closed, and no footsteps led away. I lay awake for at least another half hour and I heard not one more sound from outside. The next day I asked other people staying in the apartments if they had heard anything or been out late and they all said they hadn't."

On another hot summer night in the same apartment, Doug Keller was reading in bed when someone knocked on his door. "By the time I got out of bed, put my pants on, and opened the door, no one was there," he recalled. "I didn't think there was anything especially unusual about that, except that the next day I couldn't get anyone to admit that he or she had dropped by."

Seasonal worker Chris Summit recalls another strange incident that took place in Apartment A one winter night in the early 1980s. "I was a good friend of former chief historian Neil Mangum, who was also living on the battlefield," Chris explained. "There was quite a path in the snow between our two places, since I was always going to play video and battle games on maps with him.

"Neil generally laughed at all this supernatural business, but that winter we enjoyed telling each other scary stories. One night I left his place late and trudged back through the snow to my apartment. I went to bed as soon as I got home. With my bedroom door open, I could look into the living room adjoining the kitchen.

"I'd been asleep for a while, when suddenly I woke up," Chris continued. "At that same instant, I saw the light come on in the kitchen. Immediately, I thought of all the spooky stories Neil and I had been telling each other and I figured he had come into my apartment and was playing a trick on me.

"I got out of bed and crept to the corner of the kitchen, then I sprang out crying, 'Boo!' to scare whoever was there. But there was nobody in the room. I checked the doors, but they were all locked.

"I turned the light off and went back to bed, thinking that the light switch must have gotten stuck or something. But the next morning I examined it and discovered that it was the kind that turns either all the way on or off with a hard click. I also checked to make sure that the light bulb wasn't screwed in loosely so that a sudden vibration would make it come on."

If paranormal energy caused the light to behave strangely, it might also have been the reason for an odd occurrence in Charles and Karl Mulhair's travel trailer in 1989. An archeological dig was conducted that year at the site where Reno was believed to have dumped extra supplies after backup forces arrived on the twenty-seventh of June. An earlier excavation following a fire in 1983 had yielded much new information about Custer's battle and the soldiers who died in it, but the later dig was largely a failure. The only high point was a volunteer's discovery of a human clavicle, humerus, and skull poking from the roots of a tree along the bank of the Little Bighorn, at the precise location where the Indians forced Reno's troops across the river and up into the hills.

According to Andrew Ward's article, "The Little Bighorn," published in the April 1992 issue of American Heritage, a forensic sculptor used the skull to produce a bust of the cavalryman and the trooper's identity was narrowed to two possibilities. Although the identification is not archeologically conclusive at the time of this writing, the unfortunate soldier was almost certainly Sergeant Edward Botzer of Company G. The bust made by the forensic sculptor looked so much like Botzer's relatives that the family claimed the remains and buried them at the National Cemetery on June 23, 1991.

The Mulhairs recall the excitement at the battlefield when the soldier's remains were found. "That night, the archeologists had a little wine and cheese party to show off the skull and everybody went to see it," Charles said. "Afterward, Karol and I came back to our trailer. When she went to bed, I turned off the television and started to go back to the bedroom. Suddenly, the TV came on by itself—something it has never done at any other time before or since. We decided that the ghost of the cavalryman was trying to tell us something, but I'm not sure what it was— maybe he just wasn't finished watching the news."

One of the most uncanny occurrences ever reported at the battlefield took place in 1983 when Christine Hope was a student intern living in Apartment C. Because no one at the site knows Christine's current whereabouts, I was unable to contact her, but her story is told in "Visions of Reno Crossing," a chapter in Earl Murray's Ghosts of the Old West.

The summer season had ended and there were fewer tourists, so Chris Hope and Tim Bernardis decided that they finally had time to visit the Reno Retreat Crossing, the area where the Sioux counterattacked Reno's troops, forcing them across the river and up onto the bluffs. After finalizing plans to go the following afternoon, Chris and Tim returned to their apartments for the evening.

Chris' apartment was arranged as a small efficiency unit and she customarily slept either on the sofa or on a mattress or sleeping bag on the living room floor. In the middle of the night before she was due to visit Reno Crossing, she awoke suddenly and saw the figure of a man sitting in one of her living room chairs.

Terrified and unable to speak, Chris stared at the man for quite some time. His face was illuminated by a moonbeam shining through a window across from the couch and by its light Chris was able to make out the man's light-colored beard and long, flowing handlebar mustache. As Chris continued to study the man, she realized that he was not from the twentieth century. She had seen photographs of the men who fought in the Battle of the Little Bighorn and this man looked as if he belonged to the same era.

It began to dawn on Chris that she was seeing a ghost, but what alarmed her even more was the expression of horror on the man's face. "It was his eyes that got to me the most," Murray quotes Chris as saying. "It's hard to explain, but those eyes stood out. They were filled with incredible fright. The moon shone on them and they were filled with terror." Chris finally blinked her eyes and when she opened them again the chair was empty and the apparition was gone.

The next afternoon, as planned, she and Tim Bernardis visited the site of Reno Crossing. As they walked along the bluffs and the riverbank, Tim explained the details of the action that occurred on the day of the battle, emphasizing that those who were unscathed at the beginning of the counterattack tried to drag the dead and wounded with them up into the hills. At one spot near the Little Bighorn River, Tim and Chris paused at a lone marker with the name of Second Lieutenant Benjamin H. Hodgson inscribed on it. The marker indicated the approximate place where Hodgson's body had been found.

After their tour of Reno Crossing, Tim and Chris returned to the visitor center where they looked through an out-of-print book with pictures and military histories of the soldiers who died at the Battle of the Little Bighorn. When they came to Hodgson's photograph, Chris was unable to conceal her shock and blurted out, "That's the person I saw in my room last night!"

Earl Murray's account goes on to explain that Lieutenant Hodgson had one of the slowest and most harrowing deaths of any of the cavalrymen who died during Reno's retreat. Survivors of the battle recalled that as Hodgson forded the river, a bullet shattered his leg and killed his horse, but he was still able to grab at a stirrup kicked out at him by another soldier. Wounded and in shock, Hodgson was then dragged through the river to the other side. In spite of his agony, he tried to crawl up the steep embankment, but made it only part of the way before being shot and killed by another bullet. His body then rolled back down the bank toward the water. Murray notes that when Chris Hope learned about the fate of Lieutenant Hodgson, the man who was well liked by Reno's men and whose nickname was "Benny," she understood the tragic message his tortured eyes had been trying to convey— that what had happened to the combatants in the Battle of the Little Bighorn should never happen to human beings of any race and that no one should ever treat lightly the horror of June 25 and 26, 1876.

As Chris told her story to more people, she learned that she was not the first to have been contacted by the ghost of Lieutenant Hodgson. A few years earlier, one man had apparently seen the head of the soldier enveloped in a white gaseous cloud, which hovered over the percipient's bed the night before he too visited Reno Crossing. And according to Bob Reece, only a year after Hodgson died, his spirit had attempted to communicate with a friend, Lieutenant Clinton H. Tebbetts. This communication, which came through a medium, stated simply that the Seventh Cavalry had fought gallantly. The incident was reported by the late John M. Carroll in the November 1988 Newsletter published by the Little Bighorn Associates.

Although many weird occurrences have been reported in various buildings at the battlefield, it's hardly surprising that paranormal phenomena have also taken place at the actual sites where the fighting occurred and where the dead fell and were buried.

"The battlefield is a spooky place, especially at night," Doug Keller admitted. "The National Cemetery and the markers of the soldiers who were killed in the Battle of the Little Bighorn are very eerie and you can scare yourself easily if you have an overactive imagination."

Some might say that just such an overactive imagination was at work when a tourist from New Orleans claimed to have been transported back in time to the day of the battle, or when a cab driver from Minneapolis saw soldiers and Indians engaged in a fight to the death on a ridge. And it may be just a coincidence that the only roll of film photographer Cliff Soubier ever lost had a picture of historian Jerome Green on the battlefield, holding a Ouija board.

"If the film had been lost at the processor's, that would not have been unusual," Cliff pointed out. "But I process my own black and white shots, so I can't imagine what happened."

Cliff Nelson has worked seasonally at the battlefield since the late 1960s and although he's never experienced anything out of the ordinary himself, he knows that many of those who have are very credible people, not the type to exaggerate or to imagine things. On an evening in August 1976, for example, a no-nonsense National Park Service law enforcement officer visited the Last Stand site and, as he looked out over the mass grave where most of the dead from the battle now repose, he felt a sudden drop in temperature and heard the soft murmuring of many voices. The feeling of oppression grew so strong that he was finally forced to leave.

And then, thirteen or fourteen years ago, there was the experience of Mardell Plainfeather, a Crow and the former Plains Indian historian at the battlefield. Mardell had granted permission for a Crow medicine man to use her private sweat lodge near the river.

"It takes a long, long time to make a good sweat lodge," Mardell explained. "You have to build a fire to heat the stones and then you haul the stones to a hole in the ground to make a sauna-like effect. Native Americans use the sweat lodge to pray and to cleanse themselves spiritually, and the medicine man had a special prayer to offer that day.

"He was finished around six-thirty in the evening and he came by to say that even though he had put out the fire I should probably check later to make sure that the wind hadn't fanned the flames and restarted, a blaze. I assured him that I would, but I became interested in a TV special and forgot about checking the sweat lodge until after I had gone to bed.

"I didn't want to get up and I told myself that surely the fire was out, but I kept imagining the whole valley ablaze. Finally, I decided to make sure that everything was okay. I didn't want to leave my little girl by herself, so I woke her up and we drove down to the sweat lodge. I shone a light on the fire and, sure enough, a small flame was still flickering.

"I kicked the ground, poured dirt on the fire, and took a stick to knock it out," Mardell continued. "A lot of ash was stirred up and I knew I had to get some water on the flames, but I didn't want to get it from the river. I was alone with my child and what if I fell in?

"We drove back to the house, where I got a jug of water and took it back to douse the fire. When it was safely extinguished, I got in the car and backed out of the brush and overgrowth in front of the sweat lodge. Then, out of the corner of my eye, I saw something on top of the bluff.

"I stopped the car and turned around in my seat to look. I rolled my window down, stuck my head out, and saw clearly that something was moving up there. At first I thought that one of the summer rangers was playing a trick on me, because we were always doing that to each other.

"I didn't hear any noise, so I got out of the car to see more clearly. And there, up on the bluffs with the bright night sky behind them, were the silhouettes of two Indian warriors on horseback.

"At first I couldn't believe my eyes," Mardell continued. "For one thing, horses aren't even allowed on the battlefield. I rubbed my eyes and looked again as one of the warriors lifted himself up on his horse, moving his head from side to side to get a better look at me. One had flowing hair and the other had braids and they both wore feathers. One had a shield on his back and I could see that the other carried a spear and had a bow and quiver behind him.

"I looked inside the car and could tell that my daughter had seen the horsemen too. I jumped back in and drove home, praying all the while that we wouldn't get stuck in the brushy road. When I got home, though, I was surprised to discover how calm I felt.

"The next morning I took a cigarette and some sweet smelling sage to the place where I had seen the warriors," Mardell said. "There was nothing there that I could possibly have mistaken for two men on horseback and there was no trace of horses having been on the bluff. I offered a smoke and left the twig of sage behind."

Mardell's Crow tribe was on the Army's side during the battle and Custer even had Crow scouts. But Mardell's job at the battlefield was to explain to visitors the Sioux and Cheyenne side of the story. "I believe that the warriors just wanted to see this Crow woman who was trying to do justice to their point of view," she explained. "I believe that they appeared in order to express their approval of what I was doing."

A highly sensationalized version of Mardell's experience was published in the *National Enquirer*, but an accurate account appeared later in a *National Geographic* article. Sioux sculptor and artist R. G. Bowker read about Mardell's vision and in its honor she created a sculpture of the two warriors on horseback.

I've always had strong feelings for the battleground," Ms. Bowker told me, "and I believe there were forces working to bring all this about."

Psychics visiting the battlefield have long been aware of those forces, or at least of vibrations from the tragic past. Bob Reece writes of a moonless night in August 1987 when a psychic from Colorado visited the site for the first time. Although she knew little about the facts of the battle, she was able to provide concrete details of what occurred at Medicine Tail Ford and Nye-Cartwright Ridge. At the site of "Custer's Last Stand," she claimed to feel the presence of at least a third of the spirits from the slaughtered battalion.

Reece goes on to say that, at the cemetery, the psychic saw a ghostly warrior charge a seasonal employee, touch him to count coup, then turn and ride past the visitor center and down Cemetery Ridge. The employee had been resting, his eyes closed, but when the warrior rode past him the drowsy man reportedly opened his eyes and asked "What was that?"

Behind the seasonal workers' dwellings, the psychic also saw twenty to thirty warriors painted and dressed for war, with feathers pointed down from their heads. Reece wonders whether these might not have been the small group known as "the suicide boys," who entered the fighting when it was almost over and sacrificed themselves for the good of the people.

The most fascinating as well as the most accomplished psychic connected with the site is Howard R. Starkel, who assisted in a series of experiments with Dr. Don Rickey, former historian at the battlefield.

By means of psychometry, the practice of "reading" vibrations from inanimate objects in an attempt to learn more about the people who owned them, Starkel and Dr. Rickey have achieved astonishing results, detailed first in The Courier, a National Park Service publication, and later in the spring 1986 issue of Applied Psi.

In the Applied Psi article, "In Touch with the Past: Experiments in Psychometry at Custer Battlefield," Rickey explains the theory behind the technique:

Moments of high emotional intensity can leave their imprint on objects long after their human users have gone. Yet these objects can be like reels of old movie footage, useless without a projector. Psychometry brings object and psychic together in order to unlock the imprints of the past. The psychic serves as the projector, so to speak: he or she holds and concentrates on a tin can, a bit of shoe leather, a rusted iron spur, whatever object may have been associated with a moment of intense emotion, and projects impressions made by the passing of a previous owner.

Upon examination, psychometry doesn't seem so farfetched. A law of physics, after all, is that every living entity gives off electromagnetic field impulses, psychic traces that remain on objects even after the entity's death. In July 1979, Dr. Rickey gave Howard Starkel a rusted iron spur supposedly found in the Little Bighorn Valley somewhere in the vicinity of the battlefield. Starkel was told nothing about the spur, including where it had been found, and he knew almost nothing about the geography of the area or details about the Battle of the Little Bighorn. In fact, he had almost no knowledge of the way Indian wars were fought. And yet, by taking the spur in his hands, closing his eyes, and concentrating upon the object for five to ten seconds, Starkel spoke, giving the following information about the owner of the spur: I was hurt; this was found in a desolate area; I am with other people.... Trees were nearby, in a valley—there is emotion . . . hurry, startled, want to get on horseback, close to a stream, where all my activity was starting, trying to get to horseback. I have been hurt, and want to get across the stream to a hill to defend myself, about 150 yards away from the stream. I want to take off a black boot—I think I was shot, and am in pain but still running. . .We're just a group, but not the big group. Attackers pulled back. I am crossing the stream with a few others. The larger group is elsewhere. I am a big man, but have no hat. The people chasing me . . . one has a bull's-eye painted on his chest—they are mounted. I feel directionally disoriented. I go across the stream—this spur was lost on the south side just after I crossed the stream to climb the high ridges, in a panic to leave. I want to go across the river and north, to a main body, but can't. The enemies have backed away; they don't have time to play with us. They go back to fight the main body going to the northwest. Horses lost at the river; are there horse carcasses? I see a fire, away from the object. The owner did not make it through the battle."

Amazingly, Starkel's comments correlated with known historical information concerning Reno's retreat and they seemed to refer specifically to one J. M. DeWolf, a civilian contract surgeon who was killed east of the river at that time. Dr. Rickey points out that as a civilian, DeWolf would have had to outfit himself and thus would very likely not have worn the regulation Army brass spurs. Starkel's comments are also consistent with the fact that DeWolf's marker is about two-thirds of the way up a ridge from the river to the defense site. And Starkel's reference to a fire is consistent with historical facts, for the Indians set ablaze the grass in the valley when they left the battlefield.

Starkel was given other objects to examine, including a .50 Martin primed Army shell case. The bullet apparently had been fired by an Indian, "kneeling and shooting—not too far from water." Starkel goes on to say that the Indian was angry and grief-stricken over the recent death of his wife, for which he blamed the Army. The psychic then describes the soldiers, both mounted and on foot, milling around in a confused state with no leadership apparent. Then he narrates the actions of the Indian who fired the bullet:

"The user is not rapid firing—he doesn't have much ammunition—a careful user of ammunition. He accounted for three soldiers here—he wasn't more than 50-60 yards from the soldiers, and other Indians are up closer to the soldiers— some mounted. He was a marksman, but the recoil hurts his shoulder. . . . He has long leggins [sic] on, no feathers I can see . . . [hair] divided into three braids. Firing this weapon, there is something like a back blast—it is not like a Springfield carbine. . . . At one point, a lot of Indians leave the fighting area (the mounted men) and go northward. . . . The shell user stays in the same place or area and is still there at the end. The shell user walks away when the shooting stops—he is looking over his own casualties—scattered. Some scavenging is going on, for weapons and ammunition. An occasional shot is heard. He went through the saddle bags on a dead horse.... His shoulder is sore from shooting. The length of the battle was not long, but it was intense."

Neil Mangum, chief historian at the time the experiments were conducted, writes an afterword to the article in which he admits that reading Rickey's report about the iron spur "sent chills racing" up his spine. When Starkel actually came to the site to do further experiments, Neil Mangum was "stunned" by the psychic's high degree of accuracy, and his afterword suggests that while psychometry will never replace the standard methodology, it nevertheless has too much "inexplicable truth" to be passed off as fake and fraudulent.

Indeed, one value of psychometry is that it emphasizes the "human element" of history—the emotions, motivations, pain, and longing of real people playing their part in the unfolding of events. And no one today has a better understanding than Doug Keller of what it must have felt like to die at the Little Bighorn Battlefield. After spending at least six summers and one winter at the site, Doug has given the matter a lot of thought.

"The thing that brings about the demise of the physical body is always shocking, and dying in combat is not like dying at home or dying from an illness," he explained. "The Battle of the Little Bighorn was an extremely violent situation and there was a tremendous cultural difference involved, with European Americans fighting Native Americans. A lot of the soldiers who fought were very young, still in their teens, and many were immigrants who weren't even born in the United States. Separated from their homes and families, they must have been very lonely—and then they were suddenly and unexpectedly killed, many years before their time.

"You'd expect a certain anger, bitterness, or frustration on their part. Imagine how any of us would feel about dying young, leaving our families so early and wondering what would happen to them. If we assume that feelings can linger, it's no wonder that the battlefield is haunted."

Doug is sure that the feelings of the Sioux and Cheyenne warriors were much the same as those of the soldiers, and the Indians faced the additional threat of losing their lands, their freedoms—their entire way of life.

If there is a lesson to be learned from the events of June 1876, it's that people simply cannot afford to kill each other—the psychic cost of war is too high. This message was proclaimed cosmically, in the heavens themselves on the one hundredth anniversary of the Battle of the Little Bighorn.

Former seasonal ranger and historian Dan Martinez was commemorating the centennial with a group of historians and artists. They were riding toward Medicine Tail Coulee, a natural crossing which at the time of the battle led into the northern end of the Indian village. It's still open to question whether Custer's forces ever reached the Coulee; if they did, they disappeared into history shortly thereafter.

"The day of the centennial was rainy with strange atmospheric conditions," Dan Martinez recalled. "And as we were riding, one cloud before us literally rose up in a plume and formed into the shape of an Indian coup stick, similar to a large cane with a curved hook and feathers dangling off the end. As the warriors rode by their enemies, they would touch them, or "count coup," with the sticks. Such a custom actually demonstrated more bravery than killing their foes.

"Everybody there that day saw this shape in the sky. It hung suspended in the air, directly over the battlefield. And, suddenly, sunlight broke through the clouds and shone right on Last Stand Hill at the same moment. It was an incredible sight and everyone who saw it knew that they'd shared something special."

What was the meaning of this sign from above? Could it have appeared to show us that it takes more courage to try to understand our enemies than to kill them, no matter which side we're on? If so, then that's the most important lesson anyone could ever learn at the Little Bighorn Battlefield National Monument.

THIS PROPERTY IS CONDEMNED!

SPOOKY CONDOS AT THE BIG SKY SKI RESORT

Native Americans believe strongly that some places were never meant for human habitation and that to trespass in these areas, whether they are considered sacred or evil, is to invite disaster. A. J. Kalanick learned the wisdom of the Native Americans' belief when a routine job brought him face to face with some very eerie events in the summer of 1987.

The recording studio employing A.J. at the time had been contacted by a law firm. Some condominiums at the Big Sky ski resort north of West Yellowstone had been condemned after several years of occupation and A.J.'s job was to go inside the buildings to record the strange sounds that had been reported there.

"The builders had all kinds of problems from the very beginning," A.J. explained, "and the condos were substandard in a variety of ways. Because of faulty construction, there was so much pressure on the buildings that regular expansion and contraction from temperature changes caused them to make loud twisting sounds, so much so that anyone could tell they were unsafe. Most of these weird noises were loudest during sunrise and sunset."

In addition, there were electrical problems, the roofs leaked constantly, and the floors themselves were starting to give way. "And," A.J added, "the studs in the walls had so much weight

59

on them that if you flicked one with your finger it would sing like a guitar string."

Before the recordings could begin, A.J. had to make a trial inspection of the buildings to determine where to place the tape machines. Since he got there before the caretaker and the security officer who were to meet him, he spent some time walking around the parking lot and looking at the condemned structures.

There were two sets of buildings, each 150 to 200 yards long. The windows of the lower levels were boarded up and the one-time resort condos looked anything but inviting.

"It seemed odd standing in this empty parking lot and seeing these buildings in the middle of a mountain," A.J. recalled. "I remember thinking at the time that they seemed unnatural and out of place."

He didn't have long to contemplate the strange buildings, however, for suddenly he heard a man's voice speaking right behind him.

"What are you doing here?" it asked. Startled, A.J. whirled around and found himself face to face with a Native American.

"I wondered where in the world he had come from," A.J. said, "since I hadn't heard or seen him come up to me. He asked me again why I was there, so I explained that I was waiting for the caretaker to let me inside the building.

"'You're not supposed to be here,' the man said. So I explained that I had an appointment with someone and a job to do. The mysterious man just kept looking at me; then, finally, he spoke again. 'This is bad medicine. Go away from here.'

"That's when I told him exactly what I was going to do," A.J. said, "to record the sounds inside the condos so that those who had brought the lawsuit could go ahead and have the buildings torn down. When I explained this to my strange visitor, he finally told me what was bothering him, that the condominiums had been constructed right next to Lone Mountain, a pyramid-shaped formation that was sacred to his people. After explaining this, he handed me a small leather pouch filled with spruce needles and cedar bark.

"'Keep this with you,' he advised me. 'It will protect you.'

"I had dealt with other Native Americans in the past, and I've always respected their ways," A.J. said. "So I told him I would keep the pouch and I put it inside my pocket. And then the man just walked away."

Shortly afterward, the caretaker and the security guard showed up to escort A.J. into the building. The guard was opening the door when he suddenly admitted that he hated having to go inside.

"I asked him why," A.J. said, "and he told me that every time he was in there the furniture seemed to have been moved around. That seemed strange to me, because no one was supposed to be there."

The three men began walking through the buildings to find the best places to set up the recording machinery. A.J. was immediately impressed by the eerie atmosphere inside.

"All the doors had been left open, so you could walk in and out of every unit in the building," he recalled. "It was very weird going through all those places where people had been. Some of the tenants had moved out and taken their belongings, of course, but other rooms looked as if the people had suddenly just gotten up and abandoned everything. We even found magazines still on coffee tables and clothes still hanging in closets.

"We found the best places to set the tape recorders, locked up, and got out of there," A.J. continued. "My plan was to record from seven at night until seven in the morning and I was to go into the condos to flip the tapes or change them out every forty-five minutes.

"Everything was okay until about 7:00 P.M., when I got the creeps just thinking about walking alone through those buildings late at night. That's when I decided to call a friend to come up there and keep me company."

When A.J. and his friend finally entered the condos with only the light of a flashlight to guide their way, they both experienced a strange sensation. "It was as if we were being wrapped in a black blanket with something fluttering in front of our faces," he remembered. "And as we stood inside, we heard all the noises we had been told about. All building make shifting sounds, but these were like none we'd ever heard before. We heard creaks and pops and snaps so loud that sometimes they actually startled us and interrupted our conversation. There was also a horrible groaning, as if something were twisting and bending."

But peculiar noises weren't solely responsible for the gloomy mood of the neglected condos. Even though there had been no rain for week water cascaded down the inside walls and the steps on the stairwell were soaked through and covered with mold.

During one of the brave climbs to the second floor to attend to the recorders there, the two friends made a discovery that has mystified them ever since. "As I mentioned before," A.J. pointed out, "the noises the buildings made were very, very loud. But when we played back the tape I had just recorded, all we could hear were the sounds that we had made. The only things audible were the sounds of the door shutting as I left the building, our voices as we walked through the rooms, and our foot steps as we approached the tape recorder. Even as we stood there listening to the recording, we heard the loud sounds of the building creaking and groaning, but those noises never showed up anywhere on the tape.

The mood became even eerier at three in the morning when the two men went in to change the tapes again. "That's when we were certain that the furniture had moved," A.J. said. "The first time I had gone inspect the buildings, I noticed a couch about fifty feet from the door of the parking garage. Later I noticed that same couch sitting right near to the door. And, then, an hour and a half after that, the couch had turned around so that it was facing in the opposite direction.

"Other things had been tampered with upstairs too," he continued.

"Earlier I had walked into some rooms close to where we were recording and I noticed that all the cupboard doors were closed and some chairs were sitting around on the floor. When I looked again at three o'clock, all the cupboard doors were open and the chairs were stacked on top of each other. Even as my eyes were seeing these things, I was trying to discount them and to tell myself that I had been mistaken.

"Things started getting really spooky at this point," A.J. recalled. "Once we were standing outside again, I told my friend, 'I really don't want to go back in there.' As I said that, I shone the flashlight across the face of one of the buildings and we both suddenly froze. There, looking out at us from a window on the upper floor, was a figure.

"It looked like a man wearing a white shirt and some kind of red-colored thing on his head, but what it was we couldn't make out. We stared at him for probably fifteen seconds. We thought at first that he might have been a transient, but whatever he was, we didn't dare risk going back into that building to find out.

"We contacted the sheriff's department immediately, and they came up with a couple of squad cars. They conducted a sweep of the whole building, but they found nobody inside. The strange thing was that there was no way for anyone to get in or out of the building other than through the door we had used. There was just no other access and we would have known if anyone had gotten in or out that way."

As soon as the last recordings were completed at seven that morning, A.J. and his friend left the spooky buildings. "I turned the tapes over to the law firm, but I doubt that they were much good to anybody. The strange noises that were so loud when we were inside the buildings just weren't on the tapes," A.J. said. "I've never figured that out, since the sounds were every bit as loud as our own voices."

The story doesn't end here, however. The same day A.J. returned from making the recordings, he ran into a friend who asked him where he had been. He told her and she said, "There's—something following you around. I have a weird feeling about it." Then he told her about the Indian man who had given him the leather pouch of spruce needles and cedar bark and she said, "Go home and burn the cedar, and waft the smoke around to protect yourself against whatever it is that is following you." A.J. did so, and since his strange experience at the condemned buildings at Big Sky he has thought many times about the mysterious Native American who brought him the leather pouch for protection. Perhaps the most significant thing about this encounter is that it fits into a pattern, for on two other occasions A.J. has also been approached by unknown Indians who have helped him in some way.

"Once when I was working and teaching at Montana State in Bozeman," he explained, "I was walking across campus when a voice behind me said, 'Excuse me, sir.' I turned around, and a Native American man told me, 'You need this. Give a portion of it to your lady.' He handed me a sprig of spruce and walked away before I had a chance to question him. The strange thing was that at that time I was indeed involved in a troubled love relationship.

"The other time occurred when I was in graduate school and was having trouble with my eyesight. I had begun having double vision, sot that I had to squint, even with my glasses, to see clearly. The problem kept getting worse until finally I was seeing about seven shadowy images. I went to doctors, but they could find nothing wrong. Going to graduate school became almost impossible since I couldn't see well enough to read and had to absorb what I could just by listening in class.

"One day I was walking across campus when a Native American woman whom I'd never seen before suddenly walked up to me. Out of the blue she said, 'You're having problems with your eyesight.'

"I asked her how she knew that, but she just said, 'Never mind. You're going through a very difficult transition in your life and a lot of thing are changing. As you complete this change, your sight will come back.'

"I asked her again how she knew this, and she said, 'Just don't worry. The change is very near. You're almost complete with this cycle.' The she walked off and within two weeks my vision did come back."

How are we to explain such things as the eerie noises that failed to imprint themselves on tape and the encounters that A. J. Kalanick had with Native Americans who seemingly arrived from nowhere to help him in times of need? Some might suggest that the sounds emanating from the condemned condos had not so much to do with structural failure as with the fact that they were, as the mysterious Indian man claimed, built too close to the sacred mountain. Perhaps the sounds were not of this world at all; thus they could not break through the barriers necessary for them to register on earthly equipment. No one will ever know for sure now, since the condominiums were pulled down not long aft A.J.'s experience with them. And what of the other two Native Americans who so mysteriously appeared to him? There are those who believe that we all have our spirit guides in the world beyond this one and that many of these special helpers were Native Americans in life. When we consider A. J. Kalanick's experience, we can't help but wonder whether this might not be true.

The Gracious Lady
of the Grand Street Theater
Helena

If the folks at Helena's Grand Street Theater are right about their phantom's identity, the last thing she would want to do is to frighten anyone, especially the children who attend drama school there. For almost everyone familiar with the theater believes that the charming spirit in residence is Clara Bicknell Hodgin, a remarkable woman who had no children of her own, but who doted on the sons and daughters of other people.

Clara was the wife of the Reverend Edwin Stanton Hodgin, an early pastor of Helena's Unitarian church. One of Clara's greatest joys was putting on plays with her Sunday school classes and the church, with its stage and sloped floor, was ideal for dramatic presentations.

When Clara died suddenly and unexpectedly of a malignant abdominal tumor on January 14, 1905, she was only thirty-four years old. Her death left a void not only in Helena but in her native Humboldt, Iowa as well. Before moving to Montana in 1903, Clara had taught in the public schools of Humboldt and former students there were so grief-stricken to hear of her death that they conducted their own service of remembrance. Many even wrote to Clara's parents, describing a teacher who sang and rocked them to sleep when they were ill or tired and who took pains to understand and encourage even the worst pupils. These tributes along with others were collected in a book titled "In Memoriam: Clara Bicknell Hodgin."

Sorrowing friends in Helena raised five hundred dollars to commision another memorial, a stained-glass window designed by famous artist Louis Comfort Tiffany. Depicting a sunset in a mountain landscape suggestive of the Helena valley, the window was installed in the church 1907. There it remained until 1933, when the Unitarians donated the building to the city.

The old church was converted into the Lewis and Clark Library and the Tiffany window was removed for safekeeping and stored in the basement of the Algerian Shrine Building, now the Civic Center. Incredibly, this work of art lay forgotten and virtually unprotected in a wooden crate for forty-three years.

It might have been lying there still if Helena stained-glass worker Paul Martin had not rediscovered it in 1976. While browsing through a record of all Tiffany windows created before 1910, he was surprised to learn that one had been installed in the old Unitarian church. With the help of townspeople who remembered seeing the window when they were young, Paul Martin located Clara's memorial and had it reinstalled in its original place on December 6, 1976, only a month after the newly established Grand Street Theater had held its first production in the building.

At least one report of psychic phenomena had surfaced when the former church was a library (Cora Poe heard phantom footsteps on a staircase directly over the boiler room), but when the theater took over the old building, the paranormal activity began in earnest and soon the Grand Street Theater was one of Montana's most famous haunted locales.

While the building was being renovated for use as a theater, Jerry Schneider heard ghostly footfalls on the front stairs. What made his experience even eerier was the fact that, at the time, the stairs had been removed and were not rebuilt until a few days later. And after the new stairs were in place, Grand Streeters heard the unexplained sounds two more times before the first show opened.

Through the years, ghostly footsteps have continued to resound in the lovely old building. Mary Vollmer Morrow, an actress and managerial assistant in the late seventies and early eighties, often heard someone coming through the front door, but when she went to check she discovered that she was alone. A few years later, two sisters, Joni Rodgers and Linda Darelius, heard the phantom striding across the stage one night when they knew they were the only people in the theater.

"We were building a dragon for the kids' production of 'Five Chinese Brothers'," Joni told me, "and we were right underneath a trap door to the stage when we heard someone walking overhead. The sound wasn't muffled at all and there's no way we could have mistaken it for pipes rattling or anything else. The theater had been broken into twice before, so we went upstairs to make sure everything was okay. We didn't find anyone, so we went back to work downstairs.

"Shortly afterward, we heard someone run lightly across the stage," Joni continued. "Again we searched the entire theater, but no one was there. We were a little scared and started gathering our things to go when we heard more bumping and rustling noises overhead. We didn't want to go back upstairs to leave, so we just stepped out the door in the lower level.

In addition to her strolls around the theater in the wee hours, the ghost of the Grand Street also enjoys playing with the lights. A former director, Don McLaughlin, has a good story about something that occurred, appropriately enough, on Halloween 1985.

"I was working on the set for Frankenstein and part of it was a graveyard down stage left that stuck out into the house," he recalled. "To create a spooky effect, we used a flickering lamp and I plugged it into a cable with the dimmer off. There's no logical reason why the light should have come on when the dimmer was off, but it did. And odder still was the fact that the light stayed on even when I turned off the light board. When I left the theater that night, the flickering lamp was still on—when I came back the next morning, it had gone off. To this day, I can't explain what happened."

Costumer Aaron Haggins recalled that the lights and the radio in the costume shop have come on by themselves twice after being shut off, giving him the idea that the ghost didn't want to be left alone the theater. This motive may also explain a weird series of events on a night in the mid-1980s when Ed Noonan was trying to lock up the building to leave.

"I was stage-managing a show, so I was the last person to go," he remembered. "I secured everything upstairs and left a stage light on before going downstairs. I hadn't been working long when I heard someone, walking overhead. I went to see who it was, but I couldn't find anyone. I did notice, however, that the stage light had been turned off. I switched it back on, made sure that all the doors were locked, and returned downstairs to finish cleaning up.

"This same thing happened three times that night and, after I put the stage light back on for the third time, I was convinced that the theater had a benevolent spirit who enjoyed playing tricks on people."

Nothing in Ed Noonan's assessment contradicts what is known as Clara Bicknell Hodgin. The tributes in her memorial book refer several times to her quick wit, ready laughter, and love of humor, and Ed is not the only Grand Streeter to have been on the receiving end of her pranks.

Joni Rodgers will never forget the elaborate practical joke played on her the night after a performance of *The Velveteen Rabbit*. "I was teaching drama school for kids in kindergarten through second grade, she said. "After the play, Janet McLaughlin and I were cleaning up and getting ready to leave. Before Janet left, she reminded me to lock the doors and to turn out the backstage light.

I went backstage, turned off the light, and locked the front door," Joni continued. "Then I went to pick up the props to take them out to my car and I noticed that the backstage light was still on. I decided that I must have hit the wrong switch, so I put everything down and went to turn it off.

"When I returned to pick up the props to leave, I looked up, and guess what I saw? The backstage light was on again. I couldn't believe what was happening, so I went back to turn it off one more time. After I hit the switch, I walked onto the stage and saw the curtains moving as if the door were open and wind was blowing in. That's when I figured that Janet hadn't left after all and was playing a trick on me.

"I called out, 'Very funny, Janet! Knock it off—I need to get out of here.' I went back to the props and gathered everything up and called to her again. I didn't hear a response, but looked up to see the backstage light shining brightly.

"By this time, I was extremely annoyed," Joni confessed. "I yelled, 'Janet, cut it out! I have to go pick up my son.' I put everything down again and went to turn off the light for the third time. The curtains were still billowing and I heard a woman's laughter up in the balcony.

"I was sure that Janet was doing all of this and I was tired of being teased. I went to gather up the props and didn't even bother looking back to see whether or not the light stayed off.

"The next day when I saw her, I said, 'Very funny joke, Janet. The least you could have done was to help me carry my stuff out to the car and not make me go running back and forth ten times.' But she just looked at me strangely and said she had no idea what I was talking about. And, after all this time, Janet still swears that she had nothing to do with the weird events of that night."

Joni recalls another occasion, after a performance during the 1987 Christmas season, when the mischievous spook kept returning props to the stage just as fast as she and Marianne Adams could put them away. According to Marianne, this behavior was not unusual for the playful ghost.

"I'm sure that part of the problem was our own lack of organization," she admitted, "but sometimes things reappeared in the exact place where we'd already looked for them. And that was just a little too creepy."

One particularly uncanny occurrence in the mid-1980s still sends shivers down the spines of the folks at Grand Street. Late one night Mary Vollmer Morrow and scene designers Rick and Jackie Penrod were work-ing on stage when they heard the sound of someone turning on the power saw and cutting wood in the shop below.

"We couldn't figure out who would have been down there at that time," Rick explained. "We went downstairs to look, but there was nobody in the shop and no sign that anyone had interfered with the tools. The saw wasn't even near any wood.

"We were a bit shaken by this, so we went home. Later, we asked all the people who could possibly have been there if they'd been using the saw that night. They all denied it and we still don't have an explanation for what happened. I suppose we could have heard a sound from somewhere else but, at the time, we were sure that the noise was coming from the shop."

Because some of the strange manifestations at Grand Street have involved electrical equipment, a few people believe that the phantom is that of a man, perhaps a former janitor. If these people knew more about Clara, however, they would certainly agree that a fascination with gadgets would not have been unusual for such a progressive woman. Friends and acquaintances who wrote their tributes repeatedly mentioned Clara's brilliant intellect, unstinting capacity for hard work, and her "remarkable executive ability." Such a spirit would hardly be daunted by power tools or electric lights—in fact, she probably appreciates the improvements made on these devices since her day.

Another gizmo Clara apparently found engrossing was a fire extinguisher hanging on a wall on stage right. "I was playing Titania in A Midsummer Night's Dream five or six years ago," recalled Kathryn O'Connell. "I was standing next to the fire extinguisher, doing some warmup stretches before going back on stage. I reached my head out to stretch my back and, as I did so, that fire extinguisher began to swing like nobody's business, back and forth like a pendulum. I was really frightened, because I realized that even if there had been wind in the building, it wouldn't explain the weird motions this thing was making.

"I stared at the fire extinguisher and wondered if I were dreaming or imagining things. Finally, I spoke out loud, saying

'Stop!' Surprisingly, the movement ceased. Then I hightailed it out of there."

Kathryn remembers another strange incident that occurred when she was stage-managing a production back in the late 1970s. "I was getting ready to leave the theater and I had just locked all the doors, including the one to the shop," she said. "Suddenly, it sounded as if all the boards stored in there were falling down and then I heard someone running across the floor. Because I had just locked all the doors, the only way anyone could have gotten out of the building was right past where I was standing. But I saw nobody go by."

Mary Vollmer Morrow has heard doors opening and shutting and keys jangling on the stairwell when she knew she was alone in the theater and Jean Hardie remembers hearing "horrible creaking sounds" when she and her husband and daughter spent three nights there. "We had some expensive sound equipment at Grand Street, so for a while people took turns sleeping in the building to protect it," she explained. "As soon as the lights went off, the creaking and groaning sounds began and since we knew we were alone in the place we attributed them to the ghost. Jean's husband Pete was the technical director and, in keeping with a widespread theater tradition, he always turned on one special bulb known as the "ghost light" during productions. This tradition is commonly performed to keep phantoms at bay. "But when we were trying to sleep, the ghost light wasn't even plugged in," Jean said.

In 1990, costumer Karen Loos heard something even more startling than creaks and groans. "We were having a dress rehearsal for the play "Voice of the Prairie" and I was in no mood to be distracted by anything," she recalled. "I was downstairs in the costume storage room scrambling to find replacements for something. That's when I distinctly heard a woman's voice saying my first name, from no farther away than six inches behind my head. I spun around, but the room was empty. I went back to looking for the costume and when I started to walk up the stairway, I heard the voice call my name again.

"I searched around for whoever might have been looking for me, but I found no one," Karen continued. "I wasn't frightened, but I just turned around and said, 'Hi, ghost; I've got no time right now.'"

It was during this same play that a Carroll College student reported seeing an apparition in the theater. "After the performance was over, we left the building, and my friend told me he'd seen a ghost," said Debra Dacar, also a student at Carroll. "At first I didn't believe him, but he insisted that during the middle of the play he'd seen the white, glowing face of a woman floating up in the rafters, on the right-hand side facing the stage."

Apparitions are rare at the theater, although Kathryn O'Connell once saw a bluish white light coming down some stairs. Far more commonly reported is the feeling of an unseen presence and, although the very idea of a ghost tends to be unnerving, most of the cast and crew at Grand Street have come to regard Clara as a protective, albeit mischievous, guardian spirit.

Before knowing anything about the supposed identity of the ghost, Grace Gardiner felt sure that it was a female with a strong interest in drama. Grace has sensed Clara's presence on several occasions, mainly when she was alone in the building.

"The first night I felt her near me was six or seven years ago when I was stage-managing a show," she recalled. "Although I was by myself, I could have sworn that another person was there with me. I'm a pretty rational person, generally not one to believe in the supernatural, but I definitely had the feeling that if I turned around I'd see someone."

Grace felt frightened on this first encounter, but since then, she's gotten used to Clara. "I always have the feeling that she's slightly above me, hovering over my right shoulder," Grace explained. "I also believe that she watches our rehearsals from up in the balcony, especially when we have a small cast. I think her real interest is in putting a show together—maybe that's why she tries her hand at playing with the light board or moving things around on prop tables."

Clara has also been known to talk to actors before they go on stage and she has tapped their shoulders in the middle of a performance. And, according to Aaron Haggins, one former costumer felt someone step on the hem of her long dress as she walked across the stage. From time to time, this same woman often felt a mysterious cold spot on the back stairway near where the pastor's office used to be.

Like Grace Gardiner, Sidney Poole has stage-managed several shows and she agrees that the ghost is always fun-loving, never threatening. "I'm very comfortable with the idea of guardian spirits," said Sidney, "and the fact that one seems to reside in our theater should be comforting not scary."

Sidney has felt the presence of Clara on several occasions, but she has experienced only one thing out of the ordinary. "I knocked a 'wet paint' sign to the floor when I entered what we call the dungeon, our prop room under the front steps," she explained. "When I left the furnace room, I found the sign on the bench next to the door and I have no idea how it got there."

Sidney's thirteen-year-old son Dan also felt the watchful presence of the phantom when he attended the Grand Street Theater School of Dance and Marianne Adams even credits Clara with helping her to give up smoking.

"In the summer of 1987 I spent a lot of time by myself in the theater, she said, "and whenever I tried to light a cigarette, my match didn't just sputter out—somebody seemed to blow it out. This happened more than ten times and it finally dawned on me that the ghost was trying to make me quit smoking.

"This and other experiences have led me to believe that the spirit has maternal feelings for the people at Grand Street, especially for the kids who come here," Marianne continued. "During the 1990 Christmas season, a two-year-old girl was tagging along with me, when she realize that she had lost her sweater. I remembered that she'd had it on earlier and we searched everywhere and still couldn't find it. Finally, I looked inside the girl's toy pack and there was the sweater, folded neatly. I asked around, but no one in the theater had placed it there. And obviously, it was folded far too perfectly for a two-year-old to have done it herself."

It seems ludicrous for anyone to be afraid of such a gentle, motherly spirit, but the common prejudice against ghosts is that, if they exist at all, they must be frightening, especially to small children. Such an attitude must bother the kindhearted Clara, who labored all her short life to bring knowledge, beauty, and humor into the lives of young people. And even though she has passed from this world to the next, who can blame her if from time to time she returns to enjoy her Tiffany window and to visit the scene of so many earthly delights.

Spooks Galore
in Mining City Mansions
Butte

The mining city of Butte, Montana, has more than its share of spook-ridden houses, but that's only to be expected in a city as vital to the development of the West. In many ways, the history of Butte is the history of Montana itself, so it's no wonder that the spirit of some who developed the town named for the "Richest Hill on Earth" should still choose to reside there.

Ghosts in general tend to have poor reputations, but some of the citizens of early-day Butte are far from unwelcome in the homes they continue to inhabit. Ann Cote-Smith, who lives in Senator W. A. Clark's "Copper King" Mansion, couldn't be happier that the shade of the original owner still seems to be around.

An article that appeared in the Halloween 1979 edition of Butte's *Montana Standard* doesn't do justice to the benevolent spirit who watches over the living residents of the Copper King Mansion. Titled "Shades of Amityville stalk Mining City homes," the story by Andrea McCormick, likens the phenomena at the Clark Mansion and two other unidentified Butte homes to the horrific goings-on at the New York haunted house made famous by the book and movie, both titled *The*

Amityville Horror. At least in the case of the Copper King Mansion, the analogy does work. For as Ann Cote-Smith herself explained, "I feel safer here the I would inside the Rock of Gibraltar."

The thirty-two-room red brick Victorian showplace at 219 W. Granite took four years to build and was finally finished in 1888. Ann has lived in the house, now a restaurant and a bed and breakfast establishment, since her mother purchased it from the bishop of Helena 1952.

"The house has a wonderful presence in it," Ann insisted. "The Copper King Mansion was a convent for seventeen years and during that time a mass was said here every day. The nuns had a chapel in the house and we have one too, although not in the same room. We accumulated so many religious articles from various churches here in Butte that we needed a larger room, so we moved the chapel into an upstairs area right off the ballroom.

"I think that the existence of the chapel might be what gives us this wonderful feeling of protection," Ann explained, "both for the people in the house and the house itself. I'm a person who is leery of staying in a motel by myself in a strange town, but I'm never afraid here, even when I'm the only person at home. Only good things have happened here; the Copper King Mansion has brought a lot of joy to many people, not only to the ones who have lived here, but to visitors who come for tours or for dinner or to spend the night.

"I've talked to guests who have told me, 'This is the happiest place; there's so much joy in the house itself.' And even though there have always been rumors that the Copper King Mansion is haunted, we know that we have a very friendly ghost."

As the *Montana Standard* article indicates, the game room in the mansion stays dark and cold no matter how bright the lights are or how high the heat is turned up. "This room is always chilly and that seems strange," Ann admitted to me. "We keep the temperature in the house at seventy-eight degrees, but it never seems to get above sixty-eight in the game room. Also, there's a bathroom off this room and tour guides tell me that they can never keep the door to it open. They keep propping it to stay ajar, but it's always closed when they return."

On other occasions doors that have been left open will be found locked and lights turned off the night before have been discovered on again the next morning. Ann has also heard footsteps on the stairs when no one was there.

The master bedroom where she sleeps is directly over the dining room and tour groups walking on the bedroom floor often cause a tinkling of the crystal chandelier below. "But sometimes this occurs when nobody is upstairs," Ann explained, "and we always blame the ghost. I had a wonderful friend who lived with me for several years before she died and whenever the chandelier would tinkle or any other unusual thing would happen, she'd look over her shoulder and say, "Come on now W.A. We don't need any of this foolishness today—we've got too much work to do."

Occasionally Ann's tiny poodle, only a foot and a half high, runs to a room and barks for no obvious reason, but Ann's daughter Clancy Stockham attributes the dog's behavior to its keen sense of hearing, rather than to any psychic phenomena.

Clancy grew up in the mansion, moved away when she reached adulthood, and returned to live with her mother just a couple of years ago. Clancy likens the kindly presence in the house to a guardian angel, but she added, "I certainly can understand why tour guides and people who don't live here can become spooked, because we have a hot water radiator system that hisses and clangs and bangs. It sounds like a regular symphony when the furnace goes on."

Clancy also thinks that people expect big houses to be haunted. "We have so many rooms here that people wonder about what may be going on in different parts of the house that they can't see," she said. "There's something about large homes that makes people nervous."

A man named Ken, who is still employed by Ann Cote-Smith who lived in the mansion for several years, is apparently the only person who has actually seen the ghost and even on those occasions he has witnessed only quick glimpses of something white. "There's definitely a spirit in this house," he said. "I can feel it and sometimes I see flashes of shadow or a light-colored thing that floats and moves around. I've seen it in the basement, as well as on the first floor, but I've never seen it on the second or third floor. I did see it once on the second stair landing and, as I was watching, it moved up a little bit so that I couldn't see it anymore.

"I believe that it's the spirit of W. A. Clark and he's just checking his house to make sure it's safe and sound," Ken added. "And whenever I see the apparition, I take it as an omen that I'm going to have a good day, and I usually do."

Ann Cote-Smith invites all ghost aficionados to check out the happy phantom for themselves. "They can stop by for dinner," she said, "and if they tell us they're interested in spooks, we'll see if we can rustle one up for them."

Other spirits who are equally welcome in their old abode are those at the Hennessy Mansion, currently the home of Tom and Beverly George. The gorgeous house on the corner of Park and Excelsior was built in the early years of the twentieth century by D. J. Hennessy, founder of the Hennessy department store chain. Several families succeeded the original owners in the mansion and the structure also served at different times as a dormitory for nursing students at the Catholic hospital and as a fraternity house for students at the Montana College of Mineral Science and Technology. The Georges moved into the home about sixteen years ago and since then have put a lot of effort into restoring the mansion to its former grandeur.

Their friend Patrick Judd believes that the most commonly encountered ghost in the house is none other than D. J. Hennessy himself and that his presence shows his curiosity about the work the Georges have done. "The house was severely damaged when my friends bought it," Patrick explained. "The fraternity boys had no respect for the place at all and they trashed it badly. They got drunk and knocked the spindles out of the staircases and burned them in the fireplace. I don't know if they encountered the ghost or not, but very soon after the Georges bought the place, we realized that a mysterious male presence was still here.

"I think Mr. Hennessy was just waiting for someone to come along who would love the house and take proper care of it," Patrick said. "He got to enjoy the mansion for such a short time before he died suddenly and my guess is that he wasn't ready to leave."

Pat has never seen Hennessy's spirit, but he has sensed its presence on several occasions. "The house has four stories, including a full basement (with hardwood floors) that doubled as a ballroom and gymnasium," he explained. "It's not a dark, dingy basement at all; it has windows on two sides, so it's a relatively bright place. The sense of Mr. Hennessy's presence is strongest when you come down the staircase leading to the gym and around the corner to an enclosed landing. Here, windows look into the workout room and at this spot the feeling is most intense. It's not a frightening sensation and you don't feel it all the time, but it's fairly common.

"About a year after the Georges moved in, I was in the house sitting for them while they were on a trip," Pat remembered. "They shipped a big van full of antique French and Spanish furniture to the mansion and I told the movers to place the pieces in various spots around the rooms where they would be safe for the time being.

"Tom and Beverly called to tell me they would be home the next day, so I started dusting and doing some work in the kitchen. All of a sudden, I got goose bumps on the back of my neck and I sensed that someone was standing at the kitchen door at the top of the staircase.

"At first I tried to ignore the feeling, but it kept getting stronger and stronger. This went on for about twenty minutes, until finally I got angry. I said, 'Mr. Hennessy, leave me alone— I've got work to do.' Then I slammed the kitchen door and that was the end of it.

"I didn't say anything to the Georges when they got home, but I returned for a visit the day after they came back," Pat continued. "We were sitting there talking when Mrs. George asked me, 'By the way, when did Mr. Hennessy start coming up from the basement?' She told me that she had gotten up in the middle of the night to get something to drink and the presence had been in the downstairs hallway.

"I told her that he must have been curious about what was going on in the house, because until all this museum quality furniture arrived, he had just stayed down in the gymnasium," Pat said. "He seemed to spend quite a lot of time exploring the house after that. Every time a new restoration project was finished, he'd come to check it out. I believe he's content that someone is finally trying to put the house back together, because he hasn't come up from the basement for quite a while now. I haven't felt the presence for over a year."

Pat added that Mrs. George has encountered both Mr. Hennessy and the other spirit in the house, but she didn't want to talk about her experiences. No one is sure who the other ghost is, but it is definitely that of a woman and she has a long history in the mansion.

"After the Hennessy family left, at some time another family bought the house," Pat said. "Their daughters would be very elderly now, if they're still living, but the story is that they sometimes woke up to see the lady ghost sitting on the end of their bed, just watching them. She always appeared in a bedroom on the second floor and that's where Mrs. George encountered her too. The phantom apparently has never tried to communicate and she doesn't seem unhappy—she just appears. She might be Mrs. Hennessy, but no one knows for sure, and not even the little girls were frightened of her."

In contrast to the benign spirits of the Copper King and Hennessy mansions, others haunt selected homes around Butte. Patrick Judd remembers having some particularly unpleasant feelings at the home of some friends whom he didn't want to name.

"I'm not sure, in fact, that what I encountered was actually a ghost," he explained. "Instead, it might have been a kind of trap of negative emotions. But these friends of mine had bought an old home on the West Side, below Park Street. It was just a few blocks from the Hennessy Mansion and I would guess the house was built sometime between 1905 and 1915. The main floor is a stone structure and the second and third stories are clapboard.

"My friends moved in and immediately began redecorating the interior," Patrick continued. "When they finished making it beautiful, the had a dinner party and invited several friends over to see the house. Right away, I could tell that the woman was not happy there. While she was giving us a tour, she pulled me aside and said, 'Come here. I want you to see something.'

"She took me up to the third floor nursery area and right at the top of the third floor staircase was a small landing about four feet square," Pat explained. "On the right were two steps up into what had been the nanny's bedroom and on the left were two steps up to the suite of rooms that had belonged to the children.

"My hostess didn't say anything, but as soon as I got to the third floor landing I felt something almost like a physical blow, as if someone were trying to push me down the stairs. That seemed very strange, but I decided that I had been mistaken and that I had just lost my balance. My friend went on to show me the upstairs and then she took me back to the bottom of the third floor staircase where there was a door in what had been a kind of office. Under the staircase is a closet and my friend told me to go into the room and then to look in the closet. I noticed that she didn't accompany me.

"No one had even mentioned anything about ghosts, but as soon as I opened the closet door I felt a deep but inexplicable despair. I walked out of there and said only that it was a nice room.

"My friend took one look at me and asked, 'You felt it, too, didn't you?'

"I said, 'What do you mean—the closet? And at the top of the stairs?'

"She said, 'Yes. I can't stand it. We're going to sell this place.'

"My friend did some research and discovered that all the members of the family who had built the house were apparently still living. But when the children were little, their father had been extremely abusive," Pat explained. "He threw them down the staircase and locked them in the closet for days on end. I believe that he is dead now, but at one time he was a respected Butte doctor. It seems that he and his children must have left an incredible amount of energy on the staircase and in the closet. My friend said that on four or five occasions she too had felt something grab her and try to shove her down the stairs. Oddly enough, her children never experienced this and neither did her husband. Fortunately, they were able to sell the house and move out, even though they were initially worried about finding a buyer."

No less an ordeal was experienced by the unidentified families who lived in the two homes featured alongside the Copper King Mansion in the Halloween 1979 Montana Standard article. The first house is described only as "an attractive, two-story brick home on the upper West Side." An elderly woman had died in the house only a short time before a Butte family moved in and stayed only a year or so before eerie occurrences forced them out.

At first, nothing seemed unusual except that the family's dog refused to go upstairs even if someone went with him. Then the people began hearing someone walking around upstairs when no one was there. The mother rearranged items that had belonged to the previous owner and found them later back in their original places.

The family took their troubles to the landlord, expecting to discover that he knew some secret entrance into the house and had somehow been the cause of the mysterious phenomena. But he denied that there was any hidden entryway and he claimed to know nothing about the disturbances.

In the meantime, the walking sounds continued at odd times of the day and night and no one was ever found who could be making them. The footsteps seemed to be coming from the master bedroom, which had been converted into a playroom. The children thought the room was scary and never wanted to play there and later it became the scene of an even stranger incident.

There was a collection of old irons in the kitchen, the kind that had to be heated on the stove. The family left the house one day and when they returned they found one of the irons in the playroom. It had been thrown through a plastic doll buggy belonging to one of the daughters. The girl who owned the buggy blamed one of her sisters, who in turn swore that she was innocent.

The phenomena in the house became even more frightening one evening when the mother and three daughters were watching television. The dog began whining and pacing and at the same time the walking sounds started upstairs. The pace of the footsteps became faster and faster and louder and louder, without letting up. Finally, the children were so terrified that their mother took them to the home of a relative. The mother and the children's grandfather returned to the house to search from the attic to the basement for the source of the noise, but they found nothing. All the while, the frantic walking continued.

The family was also plagued by windows and doors that opened and closed for no reason and they finally decided to move out. But, even years after leaving the house, the mother said that she still got frightened when she thought about what had happened there.

The other house mentioned in the newspaper article was described as "an unassuming, two-story brick house on the lower West Side." It had been built around the beginning of the twentieth century by a Butte attorney and his wife and they raised three daughters there. The youngest child married, had a son, and divorced, before moving back in with her parents. She later became ill and died, as did her parents at a later date.

The house was vacant for several years until 1955, when another family bought it. The old dwelling was in need of much repair and it took this second family a year just to make it comfortable. A series of unexplained phenomena made life difficult for them, but they couldn't afford to move. They weren't able to leave for almost twenty years, until they finally sold the property in 1974.

The house, the family, and the phenomena described in this article all sound the same as those in a chapter of D. F. Curran's 1986 book *True Hauntings in Montana*. I was unable to contact Curran, but the details of the two stories are so similar that they must pertain to the same house and family. For that reason, I have combined the details of the accounts.

The unusual phenomena began occurring even before the family (given the pseudonym of "Reardon" by Curran) were able to settle into their new home. Early one Saturday morning the parents arrived with tools, paint samples, and some furniture. They had no sooner made a pot of coffee in the kitchen than they heard walking noises overhead. The footsteps continued and then descended the stairs. Believing that an intruder was in the house, Mr. and Mrs. Reardon cautiously walked to the bottom of the stairs, where they were shocked to find no one.

The phantom footsteps were to trouble the Reardons for the rest of their stay in the house. Two daughters shared an upstairs bedroom across from an attic area and one night while they were in the living room they heard the walking begin in the attic. The attic door opened and closed and the footsteps continued down the stairs and into the kitchen. The pantry door and then the swinging door into the dining room were opened, and the dog began growling, seeming to watch as someone invisible crossed the room. The walking continued into the hall off the dining room and when the door to the master bedroom flew open the girls ran outside in terror.

On another occasion after the Reardons were in bed, the footsteps and door-closing routine started in the kitchen and the sounds of a man's heavy footsteps proceeded quickly up the stairs, accompanied by the noise of jingling keys or coins. Both the mother and one of the daughters heard the sounds, but when they switched on the lights they could see no one.

Another spooky incident occurred when the Reardons held a party in the dining room. Suddenly, something turned off the light switch, making the room completely dark. A mysterious scent of flowers was in the air and the doors began opening and closing for no apparent reason. At the same time, the Reardons and their guests all heard the sounds of footsteps in the attic and the upstairs bedroom.

Also unaccounted for were frequent knocking sounds on the bathroom walls and on doors and windows, witnessed by many family members. One day the front door opened and closed on its own and both this door and the storm door, which had been locked, were found unlocked afterward. There was also the occasional smell of pipe tobacco, even though none of the family smoked a pipe, and the dog continued to growl and watch figures that were invisible to the people. Sometimes the thermostat would be turned way up high and everyone denied tampering with it.

Strangest of all was a Christmas card with five dollars that disappeared from the tree. In spite of a family search, the card was not found until many months later, when it reappeared, the money intact, in an unused writing desk in the attic.

Once in the middle of the night, Mr. Reardon awoke to see the figure of a man standing at the foot of his bed, wearing a strange costume and reeking of pipe tobacco. The phantom reached out to touch the man's feet through the blankets. At the same time, a cold draft filled the room. Experiences similar to this were to happen many times to the Reardons, who was also occasionally awakened by a tapping on his leg.

One of the daughters was awakened in the same bedroom by a slap across her cheeks and, at another time, her sister was poked in the ribs, then punched in the face.

This sister and her first husband stayed in the room in later years and the husband claimed that he had awakened to see a man wearing what looked like a pilgrim's cap, a cape, and a sword. His wife didn't believe him until a next-door neighbor who heard the description said that it sounded very much like the costume worn by the original owner who belonged to the Knights Templar.

If the unpleasant spirit in the Reardons' house was truly that former owner, they never learned why he wanted to torment them. It is perhaps significant, however, that in many ways the two families were strikingly similar. Each had three daughters and, in each case, they had married, given birth to a son, divorced, and returned home. The deed to the house explained how much the first family had loved their grandson and it stated explicitly that their former son-in-law was to be denied any claim to the boy. The Reardons felt equally strongly about their grandchild and they too wanted to keep their ex-son-in-law away from him.

Remarkable as the similarities between the two families are, they don't appear to be reason enough for the eerie phenomena in the house. The Reardons at one time held a seance in their kitchen, bringing a picture of the former owner down from the attic. A chill descended on the family and a man in dark clothing began moving toward them. Terrified, the Reardons snapped on the lights, causing both the cold feeling and the ghost to disappear instantly.

D. F. Curran's account mentions another incident that may not have been caused by paranormal phenomena. Mr. and Mrs. Reardon were getting ready to go to a meeting one night when Mrs. Reardon became ill and lay down on the couch. She was unable to move or to speak and her body became cold and numb. Her frantic husband was unable to get a response from her, but she heard everything he said. The woman's strange paralysis ended after an hour and she apparently suffered no further effects. The ghost may conceivably have been to blame in this episode, but it seems more likely that Mrs. Reardon may have suffered some kind of stroke.

Desperate to get away from all the weird manifestations, the family finally sold their home after ten unsuccessful attempts. They found a buyer only after locking hands and praying that someone would relieve them of the property.

A week later the house and all its problems belonged to new owners. Curran's account claims that since the Reardons sold it, no one has been able to stay in the house for any length of time.

In a city such as Butte where so much history has been played out, there are probably ten times more haunted houses than are presented in this chapter. In fact, one frustration of trying to put together a collection of ghost stories is that often the best ones go unreported or, even if someone does make them public, the facts are elusive and practically impossible to confirm.

One story told to me by Tim Gordon, whose other experiences are described elsewhere in this book, is too good not to include, even though there was no way to verify it.

Tim and one of his brothers were spending the day in Butte looking for antiques and one of the places they stopped was an older two-story house; the woman living there had responded to Tim's ad in the newspaper. The lower floor of her home had been made into an apartment and she augmented her income from this rental. At that particular time, no one was living in the apartment and, after buying antiques upstairs, Tim asked whether she had anything to sell downstairs.

"She took us down there and we saw a beautiful Victorian hobby horse," Tim explained. "It was a very desirable piece, easily worth several hundred dollars. We asked her if she would sell it, and she refused. We started making offers and got up to quite a high figure when she suddenly admitted that it wasn't for sale.

"By this time, we'd developed quite a rapport with her, so she told us the story connected with the hobby horse. She didn't tell us how she had come to own it, but she said that whenever anyone tried to take it out of the apartment, the sound of a child crying could be heard coming from the basement.

"Her story struck me as being absolutely true," Tim concluded, "especially since it was clear that she wouldn't sell the hobby horse for any price."

Who was the mysterious ghostly child who cried whenever the toy was was removed from the house? We'll probably never know the details surrounding this charming story, but it too lingers as a legacy of the Mining City's prosperous and turbulent past.

The Man in the Photograph

Great Falls

One of the leading theories about hauntings is that impressions of events that trigger strong emotions are somehow recorded on the physical environment: on the walls and floors of buildings or on objects in nature such as trees and stones. Then, according to this same theory, when the conditions are right, these same recorded impressions are somehow "replayed"—often to the horror of any living person unlucky enough to be present at the time.

If this theory is correct, we would all do well to check out the past history of any home we are thinking of buying or renting, and we might be especially wise not to move into any dwelling in which violence has occurred.

Emma Huntsman, known to friends as "Gidget," wasn't thinking of any such thing in the early 1970s when she decided to fix up the big white two-story house down the street from where she had been living in the southwest part of Great Falls.

"My landlord was selling the house where I was, and this other place, built around the turn of the century, was empty," Gidget explained. "I figured it could be a really nice home if it were cleaned up and all the old junk in it was thrown away. So the landlord and I made an agreement that I would tidy up the place in exchange for the first month's rent."

No sooner had Gidget and her two children, seven-year-old Tanya and five-year-old Doyle, begun the cleanup when a neighbor from next door came by to express her concern.

'Are you going to move in here?' she asked, and when we said we were, she warned us, 'Well, there are some really weird things happening in this house.' Then she said that two women had died there and that the cause of death of one of them was uncertain. The woman had been found dead in the house, and although the coroner had apparently claimed that she died of natural causes a lot of people seemed to think that her husband had murdered her, perhaps by strangling. And neighbors had sometimes heard the sounds of a woman crying inside the house when there was clearly no one there.

"I told the neighbor that I didn't believe in any such thing as a haunted house and that the speculation about the deaths was just hearsay, anyway. But the neighbor insisted again that some very odd things had happened there.

"The kids and I went ahead and cleaned the place up and then we moved in," Gidget continued. "While clearing out some junk from my bedroom upstairs, I discovered a door in the closet that led into an adjoining attic. The door fastened with a hook and eye, so I hooked it shut and told the kids to leave it that way and to stay out of the attic. It was an old house that had suffered some neglect, and I was afraid that they might hurt themselves by falling through the ceiling.

"Later, many times when I went upstairs I found the door to the attic open. I blamed the kids and threatened to punish them, but they always swore up and down that they weren't the ones who had unlocked it. This happened so often that one time I bent the hook around so that couldn't be removed from the eye without using pliers. But even that didn't solve the problem, and we still found the door open from time to time.

"Another odd thing about that house was that a person could stand directly in front of the heater when it was on and still feel so much cold that it was like being outdoors," Gidget recalled. "It was absolutely chilling. This cold wind seemed to blow through the house, and often when I told the kids to shut the door we found that it had been closed all the time."

In addition to breezes that came from nowhere and a door that wouldn't stay shut, the family was also troubled by an upstairs light that would turn itself on in the wee hours.

"For a while, we didn't realize what was happening," Gidget said. The upstairs was cold in the winter and the kids had become too scared to sleep there anyway, so most of the time we all slept downstairs. One afternoon when I was outside, a neighbor asked if we were okay. I assured him that we were, and he told me that the reason for his concern was that he'd seen the bedroom light on upstairs at about two o'clock that morning and he wondered if anybody had been sick.

"I told him that he must have been mistaken, that we had all been asleep downstairs, and that, anyway, there would be no reason for anyone to turn on that light at such an ungodly hour. Then the neighbor just shrugged and said, 'Well, this isn't the first time I've seen it on in the middle of the night. I've seen it several different times, in fact.' "

During this period, Gidget was working at the NCO club at Malmstrom Air Force Base on weekend nights and attending school in the daytime. In one of her classes she had met a friend who eventually decide to move in with her.

"My son was sleeping with me most of the time, anyway," Gidget explained, "so Linda went ahead and moved into his room. One time she told me that she had experienced a strange sensation when she was up there, but I tried to reassure her that nothing was wrong and that she would be perfectly safe."

One night, however, Gidget arrived home from work to find her new friend downstairs, trying to sleep on a cot in the music room. "I asked her what she was doing down there and she told me in no uncertain terms, 'I'm not sleeping up there. There are weird things going on in that place. The floors squeak, the light comes on when there's nobody around, and that room just gives me the creeps.'

"I tried to reassure her again, to tell her that nothing was wrong," Gidget recalled. "I was standing in front of the heater, just starting pull off my shirt to get ready for bed. And then I looked up just in time to see the upstairs light come on.

"I didn't see how she could have done it, but I asked her anyway 'Linda, did you turn on that light upstairs?' And she said, 'No, I told you—there are some weird things happening up there.'

"Next I asked her where the kids were and she said that they decided to sleep upstairs that night. Well, naturally, I figured that either Tanya or Doyle had turned on the light, but when I went up there to check, they were both sound asleep. I woke them up and made them go downstairs and get into bed with me.

"As we were lying there trying to get to sleep, we could all hear the wooden ceiling creaking, just as if someone were walking back and forth up there on the floor of the bedroom. That made me even more nervous so I got out of bed and went up to check to make sure nobody was there," Gidget said. "Of course, nobody was, so I went back to bed. But the creaking started once more, sounding just like somebody walking around. I really scared this time so I called a friend who was an MP out at the base. The MP came over and checked the house and even made sure that there were no footprints in the snow leading to it. Then I locked and nailed the window to the attic so that there was no possible way for anyone to break in. But I don't see how anyone could have done that anyway because three little wooden eaves across the porch would have prevented it."

Three or four weeks later, Gidget was sitting in the kitchen finishing a letter to her mother while waiting for her tub to fill up in the adjacent bathroom.

"Suddenly I felt some very cold air blowing in on me and I yelled to the kids to shut the door. They told me that it wasn't open, but I couldn't believe it. 'There's cold air blowing in here from somewhere,' I told them. 'Are you sure that door isn't open?' Then I walked into the bathroom and saw that the window had been removed from the frame—I mean it was completely off, sitting upright against the house as if someone had placed it there deliberately. If it had fallen, it wouldn't have landed like that. Fresh snow was all around and there were no footprints or any other signs that anyone had been there. And there were no footprints on the roof either.

"I hollered at the kids to check to see if someone was in the alley or if they could find any footprints in that direction. But the only footprints there were those of the kids themselves where they had walked out, and they hadn't gone anywhere near the bathroom window."

Eventually, Gidget began to connect the unexplained phenomena with a photograph that she had found in an old trunk in a shed behind the house. The subject of the picture was a man in his twenties or thirties, and he had apparently been married in turn to each of the two women who died in the house. Behind the photograph, Gidget had found a framed painting of a charming old homestead complete with a horse, milk wagon, and chickens set against a background of mountains and trees.

"The painting is beautiful and the scene looks like somewhere I'd like to live. In fact, the house itself, the chickens out front, almost everything in that painting, looks remarkably similar, almost eerily so, to where I live now in California. But the photograph of the man bothered me. When I looked at his eyes, he seemed to be looking right back. For a long time, everywhere I went I felt that this man was with me and I began to wonder whether he was responsible for the weird things that were going on. So I hid the photograph behind the painting to get it out of my sight."

Even with the picture concealed, the eerie manifestations continued until everyone in the family decided they had had enough.

"We decided to move back to Florida," Gidget said, "and a friend of mine offered to help us save money by letting us stay at his place for a couple of weeks before we left the state. During this time, I still returned regularly to our house to pick up the mail.

"One day I had just gotten everything out of the mailbox and was getting in to my car to leave when the man who was renting the place came out and said, 'Wait a minute— I want to ask you something. I know this sounds funny, but did weird things happen to your family when you lived in this house?' Then he went on to say that he had been forced to nail shut the upstairs closet door to the attic after a mysterious woman's voice kept calling for his younger son to come up the stairs. It was as if she were trying to entice him to go up there.

"In another incident, the man's wife laid her cigarette in an ashtray and when she picked it up again she couldn't understand why it was wet on both sides. Equally strange was the way that their sons' wads of chewing gum would reappear in the ashtray after having been thrown into the garbage. This new family didn't like living with ghosts any better than we did, and they decided to leave not long after I spoke with the man." Gidget and her children moved to Florida and then to California and, fortunately, no ghostly presences followed them. Gidget returns to Montana from time to time, and whenever she's in Great Falls, curiosity prompts her to drive by her former home. Her most recent return was during Christmas 1991, and at that time the house looked deserted and the windows were boarded up.

And what became of the photograph of the man suspected of killing at least one of his wives?

"I thought I had thrown that picture away, until the back of the portrait came off and I found it there again," Gidget said. "Without realizing it, I had left it in storage with my stuff for almost a year in Florida, before I finally found a place to live. When I saw that man's face again, it gave me an eerie feeling, and I thought, 'This time, you'd better leave me alone!'"

VIRGINIA CITY, GHOST CAPITAL OF MONTANA

Professional parapsychologists should make a special trip to Virginia City, Montana to study the psychic phenomena occurring there.

The town was at one time the territorial capital, and it still seems to right as the "ghost capital" of the state, with many of its year-round and summer residents claiming that there is indeed something very different about the place.

From its earliest years as a gold-mining mecca, Virginia City has had a reputation as a violent town—during a six-month period in 1863, 198 murders took place, averaging about one a day. Many of the killings were committed by Sheriff Henry Plummer and his gang, the Road Agents, and a number of these outlaws were themselves hanged by vigilantes, either in Virginia City or Bannack.

Is it possible that the energy from this violent past is still present in the town of approximately one hundred people? This and other theories have been advanced to explain why Virginia City still seems to have more than its share of untimely deaths, especially murders, and a plethora of paranormal phenomena. Some residents with whom I spoke mentioned a high rate of alcoholism and drug abuse as factors contributing to the high mortality rate, and former chief of police Mike Gordon said that, as the last surviving western boomtown of the 1860s, Virginia City has always attracted a number of ne'er-do-wells along with honest citizens.

"It's almost was if the whole place is possessed," said Lori Evans, a former costumer with the Virginia City Players, the oldest summer-stock company in Montana. Lori has heard the theory that gold dust gets under people's skin and makes them act differently, and actress Angela Rinaldi agrees that something about the town alters behavior.

"I spent four summers working at Virginia City, from 1984 to 1988, and I saw normally mild-mannered people fly into rages or behave in destructive ways there," she explained. "When you're in the town, you can feel an incredibly strong energy, and that energy has to go somewhere."

At no time was this energy more intense than in the aftermath of a tragic accident in the summer of 1988. Actor Peter Walther clearly recall the events of that Saturday night. "I had a slight case of the flu, so I went back to my cabin to lie down for half an hour between shows," he said, "Suddenly I heard a lot of commotion outside; it turned out that, just a short distance from my cabin, some guys in a jeep had missed a curve in the road coming down from the gulch. They rolled the vehicle and one of them was pinned underneath."

This man's head and neck were crushed, and he died a slow, agonizing death because rescue workers were not able to cut him free in time. In the hours following the wreck, at least four people reported strong vibrations of anger and fear, unexplained noises, and a general feeling uneasiness near the site of the tragedy.

"You could just feel that poor kid furiously stomping around out there and refusing to accept the fact that he was dead," explained Patrick Judd, whose cabin was near where the accident had occurred. "Even my dog sensed that something was wrong, because he was unusually restless and kept growling all night."

Stacey Gordon's cabin was right next to the cabin of the man who died, and she remembers that neighborhood dogs barked frantically and ripped apart the garbage at the victim's house. "The dogs had always ignored the trash before, but that night they scattered things all over the place and made it look as if a hurricane had hit."

Virginia City has also been the scene of more traditional haunting. At least eight buildings, many of them associated with the Virginia City Players, seem rife with psychic phenomena of all kinds.

The Opera House itself has been the setting for eerie events. While A. J. Kalanick and director Bill Koch first opened the building for the 1991 season, they were baffled to see that two of the lamps suspended from the ceiling were swinging, even though no one had been in the theater for a long time. Shortly after that, A. J. and Peter Walther heard phantom footsteps when they were getting the first show, Frankenstein, ready to go. Around three or four in the morning, the theater's back door opened, and both men plainly heard someone walk into the building

"A. J. hollered hello, but there was no answer," Peter said. "We looked and saw that no one was there, and then the footsteps turned and walked back out and the door closed again. We just looked at each other and decided it was time to get out."

This was by no means the first time that A. J. had experienced unexplained phenomena in the theater. "I've often heard footsteps or laughter when I was the only one there, but the weirdest occurrence of this kind took place another morning around three o'clock," he said. "I was working on the set by

myself when I heard a deep bass voice laughing in the middle
of the house. All the lights were on and I looked around, but
I saw no one. I thought someone was playing a joke, so I
walked out to the lobby. Nobody was there, either. I walked
back through the house and when I was right in the middle of
it, I heard the same voice behind me, laughing again.

"I spun around, but no one was there," A. J. insisted. "By
this time, I'd had enough and wanted to be left alone. I resumed
working on the stage and picked up an electric drill to plug it
into the socket. I was holding one end of the cord, and even
though I was still five feet away from the outlet, I got a shock
in my hand. I dropped the drill and fled the theater
immediately. That was the first time I ever felt endangered by
any kind of psychic occurrence."

Once, when A. J. and Bill Koch were working through a
scene, Bill suddenly turned pale and announced that he'd seen
a little spectral man standing in the corner and smiling at him.
On another occasion Bill was greeted by the ghost of a dear
friend who had died three summers before. "Larry was a
seventy-six-year-old piano player from the Bale of Hay Saloon,
and for a second I saw him standing on the stage at the Opera
House," Bill said. "He wasn't trying to scare me—he just
wanted to say hello."

Bill can't attribute the same friendly motive to a phantom
that visited him in his basement apartment in the old rehearsal
hall just up the hill from the Opera House. "This was 1985,
when I was the stage manager," Bill explained. "I really got
the heebie-jeebies staying in that room. Every night before I
went to bed I pulled the stairwell door shut and locked it
with a hook and eye, and then I locked my bedroom door
with a bolt.

"One night I had just closed my eyes but hadn't fallen asleep yet when I heard the stairwell door open. There was no way anyone could have unlocked that door from the other side, but that's what happened. I heard someone walking down the stairs and over toward my bedroom. The bolted door came open easily without being forced and I heard footsteps entering my room and walking to the foot of my bed. I felt the presence of someone standing there but, when I looked, I could see no one. I felt this invisible someone sit down on the end of my bed and, just as the bed went down from the person's weight, I felt a heavy masculine hand reach over and touch my leg.

"I was absolutely terrified," Bill said. "I began saying the Lord's Prayer over and over in my mind while my heart was beating a million times a minute. Then I felt the hand leave my leg and the invisible person get up off of the bed. I heard him walk out of my room and shut the door and then I heard his footsteps ascending the stairs. Needless to say, I didn't sleep the rest of the night but just sat in bed watching the door."

A former theater director once reported unexplained knocking on the door of another basement apartment in the same building. And Gerry Roe, who now teaches drama at Rocky Mountain College in Billings stayed for a while in the old rehearsal hall in 1989 and never did get a good night's sleep.

"It was like a nightmare," he recalled. "It was almost as if something was trying to keep me awake. Of course, my anxiety might have had something to do with the fact that I was playing the demon barber who slits people's throats in Sweeney Todd."

Another haunted site well known to the Virginia City Players is the costume shop. When Lori Evans worked there, she heard that her predecessor had once felt as though she was sitting on someone's lap when she sat down in a chair to sew. Lori herself often heard phantom footsteps and a mysterious pounding, and once she heard a man clearing his throat when no one was there.

"About a week after that, I heard the same man humming, but I was alone in the shop," Lori said. "One time when Tim Gordon came looking for me, I had already gone and the lights were out. He called my name and heard a laugh, and he swore that it sounded like my voice, but of course the shop was empty."

Lori also had problems with costumes that disappeared and reappeared, usually when she was the only person in the shop. "I came across a child's dress that I'd never seen before, and when I went to show it to Angela Rinaldi, I couldn't find it," she explained. "The next time I went into the costume shop, the dress was in plain view. I tried a second time to show it to Angela, but it disappeared from the racks again."

Someone could have been playing tricks on Lori, but she doesn't think so. And it may be significant that the dress that seemed to move by itself was made for a child, because at least two people saw the ghosts of little girls in the vicinity of the costume shop.

"There's a beautiful yellow rosebush next to the shop, and one day I thought about picking some of the buds," A. J. Kalanick recalled. "But then I had the feeling that I shouldn't, and I got a sudden hunch that a little girl was buried there. Two or three weeks later, I was walking past the costume shop when I saw a blonde-haired child sitting on the porch. She looked six to eight years old and was wearing a full-length cornflower blue dress gathered around the neckline and a flat hat with a little bubble in the middle. I looked at her once and glanced away, and when I looked back there was no sign of her. I never did find out whether my hunch was correct about a child being buried near the rosebush."

Bill Koch also saw an apparition of a little girl standing beside the costume shop, but she was evidently not the one witnessed by A. J. "This one was crying her eyes out," Bill remembered, "and she seemed to be waiting for someone. She also appeared to be aware of my presence—in fact, I think I scared her. Her dark hair was braided and she was wearing a cream-colored peasant-type smock dress with flowered stitchery and long ruffled sleeves. She also wore a tiny apron. The odd thing was that she had no real color but was sepia-toned, like an old photograph. She looked very solid at first, but, as I watched her, she faded and disappeared."

Lori Evans saw a white specter on the porch of the costume shop and wonders if it might have been the ghostly nun who usually appears in some buildings known as the Bonanza House and the Bonanza Inn. "There was a nineteenth-century newspaper story about a white specter seen walking up the street at night," she said, "and I know I saw the same thing. I was staying in one of the cabins, and around three o'clock one morning I got up to go to the bathroom in the bathhouse.

"I happened to glance up the hill, and I saw a white figure sitting on the porch of the costume shop. At first I thought it was Stacey Gordon's cat, but as I kept looking I made out the small figure of a woman, or perhaps a little girl. What I saw was only an outline, a white aura, and I could clearly see that this person had one foot up on some rocks, her elbow on her knee, and her hand underneath her chin. She was very relaxed, and I could tell that she was watching me.

"I hurried in and out of the bathhouse without looking again toward the costume shop. But all the way back to my cabin I could feel the apparition watching me.

"About a week later, a piano player for one of the other companies told me that she too had seen the same white figure watching her," said Lori. "It may or may not be significant that both of us had this experience on a Monday night."

Even though Lori thought the figure might have been the ghostly nun, its small size and the fact that it was on the porch of the costume shop indicates that it may have been one of the phantom children. But since its features were indistinct, there is no way to know.

The spectral nun that Lori thought she saw, along with the other phantoms of the Bonanza House and Bonanza Inn, are some of the best-known spooks in town. According to John Ellingsen, curator of the restoration project in Virginia City, the Bonanza Inn was built to be the county courthouse. When a new courthouse was built in 1876, some nuns bought the first one and turned it into a Catholic hospital. They then built what is now the Bonanza House for a nunnery. Both structures have been used to house actors for the summer season, and they have probably been the settings for more paranormal phenomena than any other buildings in Virginia City.

One room in the Bonanza Inn was even nailed shut because of all the frightening things that occurred there. Lin Magee was a maid at the inn in the mid-1970s, and she often had problems in that room. "My boss always called the ghost Melissa because she thought it was a nice name, Lin recalled. "But what the ghost did wasn't so nice—I would hang the towels neatly and turn around again to find them all rumpled up. As soon as I put soap in the room it would disappear.

And I'd make the bed just to have someone mess it up again. And all these things happened when I was the only person in the room."

During this same period, the film "The Missouri Breaks," starring Marlon Brando and Jack Nicholson, was being shot in nearby Nevada City, and one of the crew stayed in the Bonanza Inn. "All night long he heard somebody knocking on his door and window," John Ellingsen told me, "but every time he went to check, no one was there. Finally he went out to sleep in his car. He complained the next day that his neighbors were too noisy, and that's when he learned that he'd been the only one the building. This guy was supposed to stay there a month, but he moved out promptly and got a room in Ennis."

It's unlikely that the ghostly nun was to blame for any of these disturbances, because even after death she has continued her role as a healer and a comforter of the sick. The many tales about her are all similar and, because they come from people who in many cases don't know each other, they are more convincing than the average ghost story.

When Angela Rinaldi lived in the Bonanza House, both she and her housemate encountered the phantom nun under different circumstances. "It was my first summer in Virginia City, and we were preparing to open our show," Angela remembered. "Because of the dryness and high elevation, as well as the fact that I was singing about ten hours a day, I was very hoarse and afraid that I wouldn't have a voice for opening night. The stress of worrying just made matters worse, and I tried everything I could think of to make my throat better.

"Just a couple of nights before the show was to open, I could barely talk, let alone sing. I went to bed and prayed I wouldn't let everyone down by not having a voice. As usual, my roommate and I kept the bedroom door closed because it helped to keep our room warmer.

"I fell asleep but was awakened shortly afterward by the growling of my toy poodle, Rufus," Angela continued. "I saw that the bedroom door was wide open, and that struck me as odd because it's a very heavy door and we always had to shove to get it open. As I stared at the doorway, I saw an outline of a person. It was a shadow in the shape of someone wearing a long robe or hood, with no legs showing.

"At first I wasn't sure what I was seeing, and I must have kept my eyes on the form for about thirty seconds. When I finally realized I was looking at an apparition, I got scared and closed my eyes. When I looked again, the figure was gone.

"The next day, I realized that a small miracle had occurred," Angela explained. "My voice was back and I never had problems with it again. After talking to several people about what I saw, I'm convinced that it was the ghostly nun who came back to cure my throat."

Angela's housemate, an actor named Chris, was also visited by the phantom sister after he fell on one of Virginia City's rain-slick wooden boardwalks. "He couldn't catch himself with his hands because he had them in his pockets," Angela recalled, "so he landed right on his face and broke his nose. His glasses also broke and cut his face, and he ended up needing five stitches over his eye. Even worse, he suffered a minor concussion.

"Chris insisted he felt well enough to go on stage, so we modified that night's performance so he didn't have to do a lot of moving around. As soon as the show was over he came home and went straight to bed. The rest of us were still downstairs at midnight, and we heard Chris talking up in his room. We couldn't make out what he said, but the doctor had told us he might be slightly delirious, so we weren't worried.

"The next morning Chris woke up refreshed, with his dizziness gone. He told us he'd spent an incredible night talking with Sister Theresa, who told him he was going to be fine and that she would be there to help if he needed anything.

"We all just looked at each other and didn't know what to say," Angela admitted. "Chris was a real cutup, and we didn't always take him seriously, but he finally convinced us that he was telling the truth. He said, 'I know what I saw, and whether I was delirious or not, I know I talked to her.' And we had to admit that he had a very speedy recovery and he didn't even get a scar."

The visitations of the ghostly nun helped to reassure Angela that at least some of the spooks in the Bonanza House were benign. And she desperately needed such reassurances, because strange things had begun happening the moment she drove in from Seattle.

As she brought in things from her car, the front door she'd left open kept closing itself, and the volume of her radio kept fluctuating. Later that evening, coming back from the Opera House, she was unable to open the front door even though it no longer had a lock and normally swung open with a simple turn of the handle.

"Even when I tugged and pushed, the door wouldn't open," Angela recalled. "And a light I'd left on in the living room was off. I finally decided I wasn't meant to spend that night in the house, so I went to sleep at a friend's cabin.

"After this first day, it became more and more obvious that the Bonanza House was haunted," Angela explained. "Keys disappeared from where my housemates and I had left them, and we spent a lot of time looking for things that had been moved. One night about a week after my arrival, I woke up to the sound of my roommate Maureen calling me. She had seen a man sitting on my bed, and when she sat up to observe him more closely, he evaporated into the ceiling.

"In spite of her terror, Maureen was able to describe the apparition very specifically. He was wearing wire-rimmed glasses and a shirt, ascot, trousers, and boots from the nineteenth century. He was looking blankly at her, and when she called my name, his image became wavy, as if she were seeing it under water. Then it seemed to float up and disappear."

It was Angela's turn to see the apparition next. One night she sat upright in bed, certain that something was wrong. "I looked over at Maureen, who was sleeping on her side facing me. I was just starting to lie back down again when I noticed the figure of a man lying in bed with her, next to the wall. He was on his stomach and he pushed himself up onto his hands, looked over at me, and smiled lecherously.

"I was beside myself," Angela confessed, "shaking so badly that I couldn't even call Maureen's name. When I was finally able to wake her, we compared notes and were positive we'd seen the same man. He looked real but transparent, and when I saw him, his expression was cocky and defiant. I know he meant to scare me and he did a good job."

Fortunately, neither woman saw the leering ghost again, but other types of eerie phenomena began occurring almost daily. When Angela and Maureen came home to rest at lunchtime, they often found their clothing and shoes strewn all over the bedroom; it looked as if someone had tried them on.

"Chris lived in the upstairs bedroom, and he never had his clothes tampered with, but he often heard a woman's voice calling his name from the banister," Angela explained. "Several times he came to ask what we wanted, but neither Maureen nor I had called him. This was especially irksome because it usually happened early in the morning, before any of us had gotten up."

For Angela, however, the most alarming occurrences were those involving her dog, Rufus. Many times when the small poodle walked across the living room, he yelped in pain and acted as if he had been hit or stepped on. "He hated being alone in the house," Angela said. "Sometimes when I came home, I found him barking so frantically he could barely catch his breath, so I started taking him with me everywhere.

"Once he had a bloody scab, about the size of the tip of my little finger, on top of his head. I thought maybe he had a tick embedded in his skin, but the veterinarian believed the scab to be the result of him being hit over the head with a blunt object.

"The poor thing was constantly tormented," Angela continued. "Once some people came over after a show and one skeptic in the crowd said 'If it takes all night, I'm going to stay here until I see something spooky. As soon as the words were out of his mouth, the dog went flying across the room, just as if someone had kicked him. The skeptic said, 'Okay I'm going now,' and he never came back."

Once, when Angela and Rufus were alone in the house, their afternoon nap was disturbed when the dog's rubber ball began bouncing all over the living room—apparently by itself!

Another time, after a show, Angela came home with the dog and almost fell over an invisible barrier on the porch steps. "The energy was so strong that I felt as if I'd bounced off of something," she said. " I went on into the house and began washing off my stage makeup. The water was on full blast, but I still heard someone walking down the stairs from Chris' bedroom.

"It was dark up there, and I knew that no one else was home, but I called out anyway. I got no response, so I turned the water back on. Again I heard footsteps coming down the stairs, and it sounded as if they were made by a person wearing heavy work boots. I yelled again, 'Chris, if that's you, you're not funny.' I heard two more steps and then I grabbed the dog and ran out the front door. When I got to the bar, Chris was there, and he swore he hadn't been anywhere near the house."

One day Angela was reading in the living room when she felt someone push her out of her chair. On another occasion, she saw the shadow of a hangman's noose projected onto the wall, which itself seemed to lighten from a peach shade to white. Angela insists that there were no trees or anything else near the window that could have cast a shadow, and no trick of light could have made the wall appear to change color.

When Angela's parents came to visit, they also were treated to the supernatural phenomena of the Bonanza House. Her mother reported that her bed was shaking, and neither trains nor earthquakes were to blame. And when Angela's boyfriend stayed in the house, he and Angela both had an experience that defies explanation. Each one at a different time during the night looked down toward the floor and saw what appeared to be many mattresses stacked on top of one another. No floor was visible beneath them.

"Even if we were both dreaming, why did we have the same dream?" Angela asked, adding that before she saw the mattresses, she noticed that the room seemed to have changed in appearance. "The neighbor had a floodlight in her backyard, so even at night I could see colors. That night, the walls were an ash blue, and pictures in oval wooden frames seemed to have replaced the posters I had put up. I looked around the room for a few seconds wondering if I were dreaming, but I know I was awake."

Angela's twin sister Katie also came to visit, and she's convinced that one of the entities in the Bonanza House followed her back to Seattle. "Three or four times I had what seemed like a very real dream, in which a woman wearing a flowered, old-fashioned western dress with a bustle stood in my room and smiled in a demonic way at me," Katie said. "She had brown ringlets and dark eyes and she seemed so real, especially the time she tried to strangle me. That's when I yelled for her to leave me alone, and I never saw her again."

Chris' friend Jerry lived in the upstairs room during Angela's fourth season in the Bonanza House, and he often felt an unseen someone tugging at his shirt or tapping him on the shoulder. As had Chris, he also heard a woman's voice calling his name from the stairwell.

"One night when he'd gone to bed early, he kept coming downstairs to tell us to quit bothering him," Angela recalled. "He said that someone kept calling his name, but we pleaded our innocence. About an hour after his first complaint, he came running downstairs in his underwear so scared that he hadn't even taken time to put on his bathrobe. He said that from the wall right behind the headboard of his bed he'd heard persistent knocking, as if someone were trying to get his attention. None of us could have been making the sound from downstairs, and no trees are close enough to brush against the house."

Some time later, during a dinner party, Angela took snapshots and when the prints were developed she was surprised to find one showing a reflection of a man's face in a mirror. If anyone had been reflected in the mirror, it would have been Angela herself, because she was standing right in front of it when she took the picture.

"The mystery man looked like the ghostly fellow that Maureen and I saw that first week in our bedroom," Angela claimed, "although some people thought the reflection was of Joel, the bartender. I don't agree that it looks like Joel, and I don't see how he could have appeared in the mirror anyway, because he was nowhere near me when I took the picture.

"One night we did try to find out why the Bonanza House was haunted," Angela continued. 'We used a Ouija board and we contacted a six-year-old girl who identified herself as E-L-I- before the letters became gibberish. I thought maybe she just couldn't spell and that her name might have been Elizabeth. We weren't any more enlightened about the cause of the phenomena, but after we used the Ouija board our clothes stopped being scattered around."

Angela recalled one other incident she'd heard about that took place at either the Bonanza House or the Bonanza Inn. "The story was that a woman used profanity and was slapped soundly but invisibly across the face," she said. "Everyone supposedly saw a red hand-mark appear on her skin. It's interesting to speculate that the ghostly nun was just registering her disapproval."

Phantom ladies have also been reported at another summer house for actors, the Ironrod Cabin. Taken from a settlement by the same name the cabin has long had the reputation of being haunted, although little is known of its history.

Actor Brian King was almost asleep there one night in 1977 when the door opened and closed and someone walked toward his bed. Startled, Brian jumped up and the figure vanished. When he checked the door, he found it still locked.

Brian never knew the sex of the spectral being who entered his cabin, but when Lori Evans stayed there in 1985 she saw clearly that her nocturnal guest was female. "I woke up to see what appeared to be a servant lady standing at the foot of my bed," Lori recalled. "She wore a dress with a white apron and her hair was pulled back in a bun. What I remember most vividly, though, is the weird smile on her face. I was so scared that I pulled the covers up over my head."

A. J. Kalanick stayed in the Ironrod Cabin in 1989, and his experiences were even more bizarre. One afternoon he returned to the locked cabin to find his bookcase tipped over and books scattered across the room. The next day, while he was outside talking to a friend no more than forty feet from the cabin, a wooden tape rack fell off the wall and tapes were scattered all over the floor.

"I should have heard the rack and tapes falling, but I didn't," A. J. said. "Another time, I came back to find the television on, even though I'd turned it off before I left."

But these events were just a prelude to the far more dramatic occurrences later that summer. "I was lying down for a few minutes before going to the Opera House," he explained, "when the cabin door opened and a woman in a long red Victorian dress strolled in with a German shepherd dog on a leash. She just stood there smiling at me, and when I sat up she faded away. I got up to check the door and found it locked.

"Two or three nights later, I came straight back to the cabin after the show," A. J. continued. "I had just turned the lights off and was lying in bed when the same woman in the red dress walked up to my bed from the other room.

"The odd thing was that she appeared to be illuminated. She didn't radiate light to anything else, but every detail of the woman herself was clear. She still had the dog on its leather leash, and this time I noticed that in her other hand she was holding a quill pen. She smiled at me in the same strange way as before, and when I asked her who she was, she turned and walked back into the other room before disappearing.

"About a week later, I woke up in the middle of the night and sensed that someone was in the room. I opened my eyes and saw the woman standing at the foot of the bed, smiling at me in that same odd way.

If I were an artist, I could draw a perfectly detailed picture, because this time the image remained for about fifteen seconds. The red dress was trimmed in lace and was tight under the bust, and the skirt was full under the V-shaped bodice. The woman was very pretty, with a fair complexion and high cheekbones, and she wore her light brown hair pulled back into a netted snood. She had dropped the German Shepherd's leash, but the dog was still standing next to her. In her right hand she held the quill pen, white with black shading toward the tip.

"But this time I saw something I'd never noticed before," A. J. continued. "Superimposed on top of the pen was a transparent dagger. It had a two-sided blade and a black handle with a gold top. Puzzled and alarmed, I asked the lady what she wanted, but she didn't answer—she just stood there and smiled at me. I reached over to turn on the light beside my bed and she vanished.

"I was really worried that I was going crazy, but I believed that the ghostly woman was trying to tell me something," A. J. explained. "I decided I would ask her to come back. For a week, I asked her to return, but she never did."

The ghostly lady was gone, but the psychic phenomena didn't end. One night Peter Walther was going to the community bathhouse when he saw a strange being looking in the window of A. J.'s cabin.

"It was a tall black shadowy figure on this otherwise bright night," Peter remembered. "It turned and looked at me and then looked back into the window. I just kept walking and went on into the bathhouse. On the way back to my cabin, I refused to look in the direction of A.J.'s place again until I'd gotten quite a distance away. When I did look back, the shadowy figure was still standing there."

The Lightning Splitter is another Virginia City house with a decidedly sinister reputation. Originally a brothel, the unusual structure was named for its three highly pitched gables. The gable farthest back is one of the highest points in town and is frequently struck by lightning.

Tim Gordon's brother Mike lived in the house for several years, and he admits that he never felt comfortable there, especially while working in the kitchen, which he had turned into a darkroom. "I was always particularly uneasy when I was working at the sink," Mike confessed, "feeling that I was being watched from the stairway. But the most frightening that I was being watched thing occurred one night when I was sleeping downstairs.

"I dreamed that I woke up to find that the wallpaper and furniture had been changed. I dreamed this three times, and three times I also dreamed that I awoke with a terrible pain in my back. It felt as if something were biting me, and in the dream I was reaching around to fight off my attacker. The third time I really did wake up, and the pain in my back was all too real and my hand was actually striking something solid. I felt that whatever I was hitting was made of flesh and blood, some large animal perhaps, and it didn't want to stop biting.

"I was groggy at first, but when I realized what was happening, I baled out of bed and looked for whatever had been attacking me," Mike explained. "There was no animal in the room, but I know I wasn't imagining things because there were red marks all over my back. I was completely unnerved by this experience even though I've never believed in the supernatural."

Mike wonders if his strange experience had something to do with a former inhabitant of the house with whom he had had a disagreement. This man, who was later killed in a motorcycle accident, had apparently dabbled in witchcraft and satanism, and he was one of Virginia City's most unsavory characters, proud of his reputation as a bar fighter and drug dealer. Before Mike moved into the Lightning Splitter, he argued with this disreputable fellow, who threatened that he had "left something in the house" for him. Some evidence suggests that the "something" might have left the house occasionally, because Bill Koch and Peter Walther, in two separate incidents, reported being chased one summer night by an invisible doglike creature. Both men were en route to the Lightning Splitter at the time.

When Mike's sister Vicky came to visit with her three-year-old son, the little boy kept saying that the Lightning Splitter had an evil beast upstairs. Vicky believes that her son's claim may have been more than childish imagination at work because she, too, sensed a presence in the house. "One night when we were sleeping downstairs," Vicky recalled, "I woke up and asked my son if he was awake. In my mind, I sensed the voice of a man nearby saying, 'No, but I am!'"

Tim and Stacey Gordon lived in the house after Mike, and they reported having frequent nightmares there. Stacey's dreams often involved a child, and Mike heard a rumor from someone in town that a child had, indeed, died violently at the house.

On one occasion Stacey saw what she described as a "long, white, orb-like thing" float past her in the kitchen. "I don't know what this apparition was," she said, "but it came down the stairwell, which was always cold and creepy. And when we had guests staying upstairs they often reported hearing footsteps on the landing."

One evening, while Stacey was at the theater, Tim was at home in the Lightning Splitter with his friends Pam Koch and Lori Evans. They decided to go into town for a beer, and before leaving the house Tim pulled the plug on a lamp that was flickering. It was several hours later that he mentioned unplugging the lamp to Stacey.

"She gave me a funny look and told me that there couldn't have been any light on," Tim explained, "because the bulb had been gone from the lamp for quite a while."

A little nervous about remaining in the house that night, Tim and Stacey went to visit Bill and Pam Koch. When Bill heard the latest ghost story from the Lightning Splitter, he said, "Thank God nothing weird has ever happened in this house"—and as if on cue a picture fell off of the wall.

Earlier residents of the Lightning Splitter reported seeing a phantom woman in a chair, and Tim Gordon learned that an occupant after himself had stripped the wallpaper, gone to lunch, and returned to find the wallpaper back on the walls.

For reasons still not understood, Virginia City appears to be a magnet for psychic energy, leading many who have spent time there to claim that the whole town is haunted. Even natural formations are affected, as is evident from a bizarre experience shared by Lori Evans and A. J. Kalanick.

In the summer of 1988, they experienced the same thing at the same time but in different buildings. Around three o'clock one morning, both of them awakened to an eerie moaning from outside that didn't sound as if it were coming from a person or an animal.

"I grew up on a farm," A. J. explained, "and I've heard all kinds of natural sounds, from wild animals as well as domestic ones. But this sound had an unearthly tone to it, and it seemed to surround everything. The oddest thought popped into my head—that the hills themselves were crying. At breakfast the next day, I found out that Lori Evans had heard the same weird sound and had had the same strange thought."

Is Virginia City so full of psychic energy that even the hills reverberate with it? Something very unusual is occurring there, and parapsychologists owe it to themselves to investigate this wonderland of the supernatural.

GHOSTLY GARNET

It's ironic that Garnet, the best-preserved ghost town in Montana, was never built to last. Gold miners intent on making quick fortunes weren't interested in constructing houses, stores, and saloons sturdy enough to weather the decades. Instead, they wasted little time in erecting temporary shelters, often with no foundation but the bare ground, before returning to the far more important task of extracting minerals from the surrounding mountains. For who could predict how long it would be before the rich deposits played out and it was time to move on again?

Yet, almost one hundred years after the founding of the town in 1895, quite a few of those hastily built structures remain, lovingly restored and protected by the Garnet Preservation Association and the Bureau of Land Management (BLM). Kelly's Saloon, the J. K. Wells Hotel, the blacksmith shop, several of the miners' cabins, and other buildings still stand in Garnet. Only the people who lived and worked in them have gone—but not without leaving some psychic echoes behind.

After the BLM took on the job of protecting the town from further decay and vandalism, it hired Michael Gordon to serve as caretaker during the winter of 1971-1972. For a four- or five-day period that season the temperature plummeted and held steady at thirty degrees below zero, so cold that snow took on the consistency of sugar and never packed down so that snowmobiles could travel on it.

It was on one of these bitterly cold nights that Mike heard the strains of honky-tonk music coming from one of the buildings. Believing himself to be the only person in town, he was puzzled, but he decided that some cross-country skiers or snowshoers must have come into Garnet without his knowledge. He set off in the direction of some cabins to look for them but turned back when he realized that the music was coming from somewhere else.

"I finally traced it to Kelly's Saloon, a typical false-fronted building constructed before the turn of the century," Mike explained. "It's true that extremely cold weather can alter sounds, but as I approached the saloon I had no doubt that I was hearing the noise of a rip-roaring party.

"I walked a plank from the hillside up to the back door, and the sounds got louder. I opened the door and walked onto a landing where a stairway used to be. No doubt about it— people were talking and laughing and a piano was being played. I walked over to where a railing used to be and looked down into the bar area.

"The sounds stopped as if someone had switched off a radio," he said, "and the old saloon was empty except for a few odd pieces of furniture scattered about. I realized that what I had heard did not belong to the present time, but for some reason I wasn't frightened."

Mike and a later caretaker, Kerry Moon, had never heard of one another before I began my research, but their experiences involving the saloons were uncannily alike. Kerry was the caretaker at Garnet during the mid 1970s; during his stay he enjoyed the company of Whiskers, a border collie-sheltie mix once owned by a previous caretaker who had died. One night in the middle of December 1975, Whiskers began barking and howling

"He woke me up, and that's when I heard the sounds of music and laughter coming from Kelly's Saloon," Kerry remembered. "I was worried because I thought teenagers or transients had found their way there and were having a party. Determined to evict them, I grabbed my rifle and Whiskers and I walked the eighty feet from the guard cabin to the old saloon.

"The ragtime music and voices were loud and clear, and as we go closer I could even hear glasses clinking together. But just as soon a Whiskers touched his nose to the building, all the sounds stopped.

"I couldn't believe my ears, and when I went inside to check, the old saloon was empty," Kerry confessed. "What bothered me the most was that I had definitely heard a piano playing, and there was no such thing there. In fact, Kelly's hadn't had one for years."

Kerry heard the same ghostly noises coming from the saloon on several other occasions and, whenever he attempted to investigate them, they disappeared. "They usually occurred between midnight and three A.M., he said, "but I also heard them at other times when the town was quiet. Even in the summer, the fire crew woke me up now and then to complain about the loud parties going on at Kelly's. My brother Colin and other guests heard the sounds, too. I knew there was no point in checking the saloon again, but I did so just to satisfy people. Naturally, I never found anyone inside."

Once Kerry tried to fool what he referred to as "the good-time spirits of Garnet." On a fine September afternoon he and his six-year-old son Nathan left town, then sneaked back four hours later hoping to catch the ghosts unaware.

"We were pretty sure that no living people would be in town that evening, so we thought the spooks would appreciate the quiet," he explained. "For nearly an hour we waited silently in the shadow of a big ponderosa pine, and then the clamor began. We heard just a little at first, a few laughs and some glasses clinking together. And then came the sounds of rough ragtime piano music.

"Nate asked who was making all the ruckus, so I said, 'Let's go find out.' We walked down the hill, and just as we got to the building, the noises stopped. Nate was confused and began to cry, and I felt pretty uncomfortable myself, because once again I realized that I wasn't dealing with a material threat."

An amateur scientist, Kerry has a theory that may help explain the sounds emanating from the deserted saloon. "I believe that the many crystalline formations in the Garnet Range might somehow receive radio waves and that the dense mineral deposits in the area might act as speakers," he explained. "The miners drove many long metal shafts, rods, and pipes into the quartz formations for ventilation and water removal, and these may also act as antennae. Perhaps the sounds from the saloon are resonating from this mixture of quartz, other minerals, and the metal shafts. If the town of Garnet really is a big radio receiver, the, music and voices are audible because they are real and could probably be recorded."

Kerry once tried to do just that with a microphone attached to a small tape recorder, but it picked up only background noise. He believes that better equipment probably would have recorded the sounds more clearly. "Of course, I suppose it's also possible that the music and voices really are coming to us from the past," he said. "Or perhaps the spirits of Garnet are in there celebrating their lost way of life, when the town was a booming mecca for the miners of the last Montana gold rush."

As plausible as this theory may be, Kerry has none to explain the mysterious caller whom he heard walking up to his cabin and knocking on the door just before midnight. When Kerry opened the door no one was there, and the only footprints in the snow were those leading up to the porch—but none leading away.

Unexplained footsteps are nothing new to the current caretaker of Garnet, Dwight Gappert, who has heard the sounds of walking and doors shutting inside buildings known to be empty. "For one thing, most of these old structures no longer have doors," he explained. "And one of the more frequently heard noises is that of people walking up the staircase to the second story inside the Wells Hotel. The stairway has about thirty steps, so there's a definite recognizable pattern to the footsteps. And whenever you approach the buildings, the noises stop."

Dwight said that most of the unexplained sounds he has heard occur either at daybreak or at dusk. He remembers one woman who had a very frightening experience after leaving her rental cabin just after the sun had gone down. "It was quite a jaunt from her cabin to the restroom," he recalled. "And on her way back to the cabin she noticed two people walking up the street. She called to them but they didn't answer. And then she noticed that their clothing was old-fashioned and that the gentleman was wearing bib overalls.

"She continued following them up the main street, which had only a few buildings still standing. They approached the hotel and went inside; the woman following them heard the sounds of a piano playing and people dancing.

"She ran the rest of the way back to her cabin and told her husband what had happened," Dwight said. "They grabbed a flashlight and returned to the hotel, only to find the front door locked and no sign of music or dancing."

John Ellingsen, a former curator and one of the directors of the preservation project, had his own spooky experience at the old hotel. He was taking measurements there in the summer of 1970 accompanied by a German shepherd dog belonging to John Crouch, the other director. Suddenly the dog ran frantically from the building, barking hysterically.

"At first I thought he'd probably heard a pack rat," John said, "but as I stood there and listened, I heard what sounded like human footsteps up on the top floor. The dog refused to go into the hotel after that.

"A year later, I had another scare at the same place," he continued. "I was in Garnet with a group of high school kids, and we'd spent much of the evening telling ghost stories and getting all psyched up. There were about eight of us, and we decided to take a flashlight to the hotel to see if we could find any spirits.

"It was a spooky night with the moon shining, and we walked out through the woods. The hotel was all boarded up back then, so we had to enter it through the back door. We started up the stairs with the flashlight and passed the second floor. But just as we got to the third floor, the flashlight went out.

"You should have heard all the screaming," John said, laughing. "We thought the ghost had gotten us, but a bigger danger was that somebody would fall through one of the holes in the floor. By groping along in the dark, we all got out of there in one piece.

"I had decided that the flashlight going off while we were inside the hotel was just a coincidence," John said, "until it came on again the second we walked out the door."

Al Wahlin is another person who has spent a great deal of time in Garnet, both as a summer visitor and as a former caretaker. He admitted that he has often wandered around the town late at night hoping to stir up the ghosts but having no luck. One night he thought he heard mysterious voices talking in another building, but then he realized that the sound was merely the buzzing of flies trapped between the trim and the window.

Al did experience a bona fide eerie encounter one spring day in 1978 or 1979 when the ice and snow were breaking up and melting off. "That time of year was especially nice," he said, "because usually no one came to town and I had the whole place to myself. I had been working on some project up in the shop, and I was about halfway back to my cabin when something made me glance over my shoulder.

"I saw a man, a woman, and a small child walking about thirty yards behind me. I hadn't talked to anybody for a week or two, and I was surprised to see them. I decided it would be nice to find out what they were doing in Garnet, so I turned around again to call to them—and no one was there.

"I couldn't figure out where they could have gotten to so quickly, especially as they were strolling along with the child between them, and the middle of the street was the only place where the snow was packed well enough to walk. I checked behind bushes and everywhere else I could think of, even going off on little side trails before convincing myself that I was the only person in town. And when I looked for footprints, the only ones I saw were the distinctive waffle patterns made by my own boots.

"Nothing seemed to be unusual about these people," Al insisted. "They were dressed normally for winter and they looked like a modern family, not inhabitants of early-day Garnet. The woman, for example, was wearing pants instead of a dress. I don't know who they were or how they managed to get out of sight so fast."

Al's desire to experience the unexplained at Garnet was rewarded on one other occasion, and he later learned that his wife, Gloria, had had an identical experience at the same place on a different evening. "It was winter sometime in the early 1980s," Al explained, "and we had rented a cabin known as the Dahl House. I woke up one night to see a glowing light floating over the woodstove in the center of the room. The whitish yellow light was about the size of a soccer ball, and after a while it rose to distance of about five feet and began moving toward me. Then it floated up to a corner of the room above my head and disappeared.

"I wasn't really frightened, but I was puzzled, and I know I wasn't dreaming. I didn't find out that Gloria had seen exactly the same thing in the same place until we both began talking about the odd things that happen in Garnet."

Those "odd things" certainly are well documented, for in addition to appearing in this book, Garnet has been featured in D. F. Curran's "True Hauntings in Montana" and in Earl Murray's "Ghosts of the Old West." Perhaps the ultimate irony of this town not built to last is just how permanent its ghostly inhabitants appear to be.

THE HAUNTING OF THE
MONTANA STATE UNIVERSITY THEATER

BOZEMAN

Wherever there are theaters, there are likely to be ghosts, and current theories about psychic phenomena may help to explain why. Parapsychologists know that whatever else so-called "supernatural" occurrences may be, they are definitely manifestations of energy. This energy may come from disembodied spirits or merely from residual emotions that somehow become recorded on the physical environment, to be "played back" under conditions not yet fully understood.

Is it so hard to believe, then, that the spirits of actors, directors, or others who loved the stage during their lives might choose to linger there after death? Or that all the emotional intensity produced by actors performing and audiences responding might be psychically imprinted onto the very walls or the floor and then somehow released?

Whatever theater ghosts are, Montana has more than its share. And of all the theaters in the entire state, none has a more tragic reason to be haunted than the one at Montana State University (MSU) in Bozeman.

When Chris McLaren came to MSU in the mid-1970s, she heard rumors that the theater had a ghost. She never took the stories seriously, however, until one night when she and another student stayed late to rehearse.

"Everybody had gone home except for the two of us," she remembered, "and because all the doors were locked on the outside, no one else should have had access to the building. Yet, while we were trying to concentrate on our scene, we kept hearing the sound of someone walking in the shop area behind the stage.

"There were two staircases leading from this part of the theater to the rooms downstairs," Chris explained, "and we distinctly heard footsteps going up and down the metal spiral staircase. Each time we heard the walking sounds, we went to see who was there, but we never found anyone. We even went downstairs to check the rooms below, but they, too, were empty. The sounds of the footsteps occurred so many times that we got a little spooked. Finally, we decided to leave."

What happened next has remained vivid in Chris' memory, and it definitely made her a believer in ghosts. "Before leaving, we were supposed to turn off all the lights and make sure the doors were locked behind us," she recalled. But we looked up from the stage, we saw a man in the sound booth. We couldn't imagine who he was or why he was there, but because we didn't want to lock anyone in for the night we went up to check.

"When we got there, the sound booth was empty," Chris said. "That seemed odd, but what was even more unsettling was coming back down again and seeing the same man in the same place—he hadn't moved an inch. I had never seen him before and I'll never forget what he looked like. His hair was graying and he had a beard, perhaps a goatee. He was also wearing a light-colored suit.

"Besides the fact that the sound booth was empty when we checked it," Chris said, "another problem was that even if someone had been in there, it wouldn't have been possible to see him at the window as we did. A control board was placed right against the glass, leaving such a small space that no human being could have fit there.

"After seeing the man for the second time, we just wanted to get out of that place—fast! We left without turning off one bank of lights, because there was no way we were going to walk all the way from the stage to the door in the dark. When we came back the next morning everybody asked why we'd left the lights on. We explained what had happened and one of the professors said, 'I think we'd better tell you something.'"

Chris and her friend were shaken by the bizarre and tragic tale that unfolded. About two years before Chris arrived at MSU, a man named Jon Schmidt (a pseudonym) had been director of the theater program. Brilliant and talented, he was well known and very influential in Montana dramatic circles. On one occasion he was walking down the metal spiral staircase behind the stage when he slipped on the treacherous steps and fell all the way to the bottom. The accident left him with a massive concussion.

Brain injuries of this kind sometimes create deep depressions and dramatic mood swings and, unfortunately, Jon Schmidt suffered from both. For about two weeks following the accident he grew more and more despondent. On opening night of a production, in his office right next to the sound booth, he shot himself with a prop pistol. His body was found shortly afterward by members of the sound crew.

"After telling us about how the poor fellow died, the professors asked if we'd gotten a good look at the man who had been up in the sound booth the night before," Chris continued. "I said that I had and then described him. When I finished, they looked at each other and said, 'You've just described Jon Schmidt.'

"I don't recall ever seeing any pictures of him," Chris said, "before or after we had our strange experience, and the professors were satisfied that there was probably no way we could have known what the former director looked like."

After the suicide, stories surfaced about a bloodstain marking the exact spot where Schmidt met his death. Gerry Roe, now at the drama department at Rocky Mountain College in Billings, worked at MSU from 1981 to 1987, and he inherited Schmidt's office.

"I'd heard about the suicide, of course, but at the time I had no idea that someday I would work at MSU," he explained. "When I first got there, Joel Jahnke, who is still director of the theater department, pointed out the stain to me. There's not much to it and I didn't think it would bother me. Joel continued showing me around, and a little while later I walked back around my desk and saw red spots on the floor. I totally freaked out—until I realized that Joel's little kid had drawn them there with a magic marker.

"Except for this rather shaky start, I didn't mind being in the office for the first six months," Gerry said. "But then, for some reason, it started getting to me. I couldn't stand to be alone in that room or even in the building late at night. And whenever I saw myself in the double-glass windows overlooking the theater, I was startled by my own reflection.

"I was okay if someone was with me, but that wasn't always possible. I began going into the building at six o'clock in the morning to get my work done, and nothing ever bothered me then.

"The whole time I was there, I heard a lot of talk about people experiencing strange phenomena," Gerry continued. "One night I was back in the shop area getting ready to leave the theater when I saw what seemed to be a backlighted silhouette of a man. I had just checked the doors about ten minutes before and I didn't see how it was logistically possible for anyone to have gotten in since then. I don't know if I saw a ghost or what, but I was so frightened that I took off down those curved stairs and flew out some doors into the alley. I've thought about this experience a lot since then, and I just don't know how a flesh-and-blood human being could have gotten into the building that night."

Although the tragic story of Jon Schmidt certainly seems reason enough for the MSU theater to be haunted, some accounts of ghostly phenomena there actually precede his death and point to the presence of another entity. Steve Wing, now production coordinator for drama at the University of Montana in Missoula, was working in the MSU theater in the fall of 1970, and he remembers a very strange experience that occurred late one night.

"The greenroom also doubled as a performing space, and we were doing a show there at that time," Steve explained. "We were using a piece of electronic equipment called a light organ, which casts different patterns on a plastic screen to match various sounds. The dress rehearsal had ended several hours earlier, and everything had been unplugged. A woman and I came up out of the costume shop to take a break, and we were very shocked to see the light organ come on and start pulsing. The woman stood there and watched it while I ran down to get the other people in the costume shop. When I returned with them, the thing was still pulsing.

"We double-checked the light organ, and it was definitely unplugged," Steve insisted. "There was no obvious source of electricity going into it, and we wondered if the power had somehow built up so that the capacitors were just at that time releasing it. An electrician assured us that such a thing wasn't possible after the light organ had been shut off for a long time. We never could figure out what caused the strange pulsing."

If a spirit was to blame for this odd manifestation, it obviously wasn't Schmidt's, because this incident occurred four years before his death. And although no one knows for sure how many ghostly presences are wreaking havoc at the theater, it appears that at least one of them is female.

Former student Bill Koch heard rumors that a woman had hanged herself in the ballroom of the Student Union Building, now called the Strand Student Union, in an area near what became the light room of the theater. I checked with Mildred Leigh, director of the student union from 1940 to 1968. She had never heard the rumor, and she felt sure that if such a thing had happened she would have known about it. She in turn checked with some other early-day employees of the union, and none of them believed that the story had any basis in fact.

Two sightings of an apparition are especially interesting in light of the rumor, however. Approximately five years ago, a costume student was on stage when she saw a woman standing in the house. Before the specter disappeared, the student noticed that she was clad in an evening dress from the style of the late 1920s or early 1930s. A month or two later, the student saw the apparition again, wearing the same clothing and standing in the same spot. It is intriguing to speculate whether this woman was the one reputed to have hanged herself (if, in fact, such an event ever occurred). And although it's unlikely that anyone would wear an evening gown to commit such a gruesome act, it's interesting nevertheless that a phantom dressed to go to a dance should appear near the site of the old ballroom.

Regardless of the truth of the rumor, other people have also reported eerie phenomena involving a phantom woman. A. J. Kalanick, now a full-time actor, encountered, in 1986, what he is sure was a female ghost. "I walked into the theater by myself, calling out the name of an actress with whom I was to rehearse a scene," he replied. "The theater was totally dark except for the red lights shining from a boom box stereo the actress had left on the stage. I kept calling out her name and getting no response. I walked down the aisle, and as I got to the edge of the stage I heard footsteps coming off the stairs toward me. I called the actress' name again and got no answer, but suddenly I felt some fabric brush over my arm. Thinking the actress was there after all, I reached out to grab her, and there was only empty space. I called her name again and felt a hand run down my arm, but still no one was there.

"At that point, I turned and ran like crazy out of the theater and bumped into the actress in the hall. She said I looked like I'd seen a ghost, and I told her that at least I'd touched one. Together we went back into the theater and turned on the lights. I told her that earlier the lights from her boom box had been on. "'You couldn't have seen them,' she said. 'The batteries gave out and that's why I left, to get new ones at the bookstore.'

"There's no way that the lights on her stereo could have been on, and yet they were," A. J. insisted. "And I'm not sure whose hand and arm I felt, but they definitely seemed to belong to a woman.

"Another time, during a show Gerry Roe was directing, I was standing off on the side stage when I heard a woman scream. I turned to the stage manager and asked, 'Who the heck is that?' He didn't hear it, and she screamed again. I said, 'There— did you hear that?' But he hadn't, so obviously not everyone is sensitive to these phenomena."

Pamela Jamruszka-Mencher, who now teaches drama and speech at Red Rocks Community College in Lakewood, Colorado, is one of the few people who have actually seen the ghost of a woman who appears to be an actress. "I was the costumer, so I was often there very late at night," she explained. "My office was in the front of the theater, and when it was time to leave I walked through to the back, where I parked my car. The first time I saw the phantom on stage I thought she was a friend of mine. I hollered out, 'Hi, Lisa. Why are you still here?' Then the figure turned to me before it literally disappeared right before my eyes.

"She was blonde and looked about eighteen years old," Pam remembered. "I was standing in the house and she was about forty feet away, so it was hard to make out any facial features. The dress she was wearing was a costume of some sort, and the style was from the late eighteenth or early nineteenth century. I didn't hear her say anything, but she looked as if she were performing.

"When she disappeared right in front of me, I just knew I'd stayed up too late," Pam said, laughing. "But when I saw her the second time I became convinced that she wasn't just a figment of my imagination. On this occasion I had been one of the last to leave after the initiation ceremony for the theater fraternity. I was up above the stage on the cat-walk when suddenly one of the lights came on and there was this same woman.

"This time I had the presence of mind enough not to holler," Pam said, "and I just stared at her. She was only about fifteen feet away, so I could observe her more closely. She was wearing the same dress I'd seen her in before, and her hair was piled on top of her head. She looked absolutely real and I wasn't frightened until, after about three seconds, she looked up at me and disappeared again. Now that I knew for sure I'd seen an apparition, I felt scared.

"After thinking about these two sightings over the years, I'm convinced that what I saw was the ghost of an actress playing a part," Pam explained. "There were some discrepancies in her costume, and it may well be that she was an actress in the 1940s playing someone from an earlier time."

Pam never got the feeling that the apparition was worried or upset, but a particularly eerie experience made her wonder if this spirit, or perhaps the spirit of Jon Schmidt, might have tried to contact her one evening.

"At one point I didn't have a place to live, so I ended up moving into the theater for a couple of weeks," Pam explained. "I stayed in a little area off to one side of the costume shop, under the stairs. We called this place the 'authentic room,' because it was here that we kept articles of actual clothing that were donated to be used as costumes. We had clothing from the nineteenth century, and this dry room helped to protect the fabrics.

"I made this place as comfortable as I could with a little bed, a lamp, and an aquarium with an angel fish," Pam continued. "One night I was up late studying and doing my laundry in the washing machine in the costume shop. I got up to change the clothes from the washer to the dryer, and when I came back to my room something felt strange to me. I had the feeling that someone had been there. I told myself I was just being silly, and I sat down in my chair and resumed studying.

"I always keep a notepad right next to the fish tank, and the something made me look at it," Pam said. "Just a few minutes before the sheet on top had been clean, but now I saw some spidery handwriting, a mixture of cursive and block letters that looked like the scrawling of a drunk person. Stunned, I made out the words: 'Help me, somebody. Please help me.'

"'I'd like to help you,' I said, 'but I need to know who you are.'

"I tore the note off of the pad and examined it closely. And while I was doing that, a pencil lying on the table nearby began to roll, as if someone were about to pick it up.

"This was too much—I just couldn't handle any more," Pam confessed. "I know that nothing I did made the pencil move because I wasn't even touching the table when that happened. I was so scared that I ran out of the room and fled to a local restaurant where I sat up all night. I didn't come back until dawn.

"To this day I regret that I didn't have the courage to stay," Pam said, "because now that I'm older, I tend to think psychic phenomena are fairly harmless. But I hadn't figured that out when I was nineteen. As soon as I got back to my room I checked the note pad to see if someone had written a name or a message, but there was nothing.

"At the time, I thought the woman I'd seen on stage might have been the one trying to contact me, but it might have been Jon Schmidt. I didn't know him because I entered the theater program in 1974, just two days after his death; I remember what a hard time that was for everybody. And there were definitely unseen presences in the building."

Pam, who in addition to teaching now runs the Roving Stage Theater Company with her husband, has an interesting and plausible theory about why weird occurrences take place so often in theaters: "There's so much extreme emotion in a play, and I believe that sometimes it stays around," she explained. "Sensitive people might be aware of it and perhaps even add their own energies to it to cause some kind of physical manifestation. I think we can activate things that may be lying dormant. So I don't necessarily believe that all these things are attributable to spirits."

Probably the most common type of unexplained incident at the MSU theater is the disappearing and reappearing of objects. Costume and set designer Mary Alyce Hare will never forget one such experience that defied logic.

"I was alone in the building around one o'clock in the morning working on my first production at Montana State," she remembered. "It was called "Waltz of the Toreadors," and it was to open in about a week and a half. At that time we had an oversized shoebox for storing all the buttons collected over the years, and I pulled it out and set it on the edge of our cutting table. Then I went around the corner and down the hall to the dressing room, where I picked up the smoking jacket that was to have the silver buttons.

"I returned to the costume shop and laid the jacket out on the table," Mary Alyce continued. "That's when I saw that the button box was no longer there.

"I'm a little nervous about being alone in the theater at night," she explained, "so I always make sure that all the doors to that area are locked. And on this particular night I knew I was the only person there. So even though I was sure I'd put that box on the table, I decided that I must have been mistaken and that I hadn't brought it out after all. I looked all over the shop, but I couldn't find the box anywhere. I finally got tired of searching and decided to look for it again the next day.

"When I came back, two seamstresses spent an hour with me trying to locate the button box, but we had no luck. Because this box had all the buttons we used for all the shows, we were really in a fix, and ended up having to buy buttons for the whole show.

"A few days after Waltz of the Toreadors opened, I started working on costumes for 'The Elephant Man,'" Mary Alyce continued. "Again, it was late at night, I was by myself, and everything was locked up. This time I was going to cut fabric, and I cleared everything off of the table to make room for it. I went to pick up the material, just a few feet away, and when I came back the button box was on the table, just where I had last seen it two weeks before!

"This was a most bizarre occurrence because there was absolutely no one else in the building, and even if there had been, no one could have placed that box there without my seeing or hearing it. Remember that this is a big container full of buttons that click together noisily whenever the box is moved."

In addition to playing games with the buttons, the mischievous spirit has also trifled with the costumes. "We store these in a cage that used to be kept locked," Mary Alyce explained. "Several times I've taken garments out of the cage and placed them in the costume shop, only to have them disappear. Then I've found a substitute, and after the show opened I've discovered the original costume back inside the locked cage.

"The reverse has also happened, when I enlisted the entire crew to help me search for a particular costume that I knew existed. When we didn't find it, I locked the cage and went home. When I came in the next day, I found the costume we'd been looking for hanging in plain sight on the inside of the cage door. We like to joke that at least the ghost has good taste in the clothing it takes."

Mary Alyce says that most of the people who work in the costume shop believe that the presence is female. "A co-designer of mine who often works alone says that sometimes she feels someone walking behind her, and she catches a whiff of perfume. She turns to look, figuring that somebody has entered the door, but nobody's there."

Mary Alyce wryly recalls one incident in which she blamed the ghost for something it didn't do and then suffered the spirit's wrath as a consequence. "About seven or eight years ago, when we were doing 'Shakespeare in the Park' programs, I found a pair of shoes for an actor with an odd foot size," she said. "I'd taken them in to be repaired, and then I put them in the shop. A day or two before dress rehearsal I realized that the shoes were missing. By this time the actors were working and rehearsing outside, so it was possible that the shoes had gotten lost out there. I sent one of the actresses to look for them, but she had no luck.

"I was having a really bad day and I just assumed that the ghost had taken the shoes," Mary Alyce continued. "I was all by myself, and I walked into the shoe room and hollered an unprintable version of 'Okay, lady—we've had enough. I want those shoes back—now!'

"Then I walked out of the shoe room through the cage area and into the costume shop. In literally no more than two minutes all the sewing machines started to jam up, the iron began to spew water, and a seamstress who was doing some hand-sewing felt the needle snap in two in her hand. And she wasn't working on heavy fabric, either.

"At this point, I pulled aside the other designer and told her that I'd made a big mistake—I had infuriated the ghost by yelling at her. Then I ran back into the shoe room and apologized privately to the lady herself.

"Of course, all the problems stopped immediately," Mary Alyce said with a laugh, "and about ten minutes later an actress came waltzing through the door, saying, 'I found Henry's shoes. They were underneath something on the set.' So the ghost hadn't taken them after all."

Theater director Joel Jahnke admits that some of the peculiar goings on might be attributed "to a bunch of rummy theater people running around at two in the morning." But he, too, has had an experience that defies explanation.

"I carried a board from a chair into the shop," he said. "I was looking for a clamp, and when I found it I took it out to the chair. Then I remembered that I'd set the board down in the tool room and I went back to get it. It wasn't there.

"Nobody had been anywhere near me in the shop or the tool room. I looked everywhere for that board, and later I had other people looking, too, but we never found it."

Still other unexplained phenomena have occurred at the MSU theater. In the middle of a performance, A. J. Kalanick and an actress heard someone walking directly behind them, from one side of the stage to the other, when it was obvious that no one was there. A. J. also recalls walking up the metal spiral staircase with two other men when the center pole seemed to "explode with light." He has never been able to explain what happened, but admitted, "We couldn't get off those stairs fast enough."

Another student, Stacey Gordon, often saw tiny blue flashing lights in the rafters of the greenroom, and she was on stage during a performance of "The House of Blue Leaves" when the sound of an explosion failed to take place as planned. The crew then slammed two doors to create the desired effect, but when the cast tried to go through the doors to the backstage area during intermission, they seemed to be glued shut. "They weren't just stuck—they absolutely wouldn't budge," Stacey recalled. "We had a football player in the cast who tried to pull one door open, but even he couldn't do it. Later, it opened easily, without being forced at all."

On another occasion, Stacey was playing one of the witches in the "unlucky play," "Macbeth." She entered the stage during a performance and realized too late that she'd left her street shoes on. "I didn't want to turn around and walk off, so I tried to back into the hole where I'd come out," she explained. "I missed my mark, and at the same time a guy fell on me, hitting me in the head and knocking me unconscious.

"I honestly don't remember anything else, except that when I came to I found myself in the hole where I was supposed to be, safely underneath the stage," Stacey said. "I don't know how I got into it, because there's no way I could have crawled there. I think someone or something must have guided me."

Not everyone has felt so secure in the presence of the phantoms. Bill Koch, for example, was frightened by a strange sequence of events that took place after he received the Jon Schmidt theater scholarship in the early 1980s. "I never believed in ghosts before I went to MSU," he explained, "but

I knew the legend that everyone receiving the scholarship would eventually encounter the spirit of the former director.

"I just laughed at that idea until late one night in July. I'd been working downstairs in the prop room, and when I went upstairs to lock everything up I felt as if ninety pairs of eyes were watching me. I stood on stage for a minute and called out, 'Hello, who's in here?'

"I didn't see how anyone could have gotten into the building because the front doors were locked and secured with safety bars. And yet I had the strangest feeling that I was not alone. As I stood on the stage, the area around me seemed to get darker, and when I went into the shop the window in the door looked as if it were fogged over, even though it was a sunny day. I had such a bad feeling that I backed down the stairwell and ran out of the building, not even bothering to lock the door behind me."

Bill's next weird experience took place the second week of August, when he was painting one of the makeup rooms. "Suddenly, I heard footsteps up above in the shop," he said. "I couldn't figure out who it was or how anyone could have gotten in because the front doors were locked, and I would have seen anyone who entered through the open back door.

"As I stood there listening for more footsteps, I heard the sound of the table saw starting up. That really annoyed me because I was in charge of the building, and no one else should have been in it. I started up the spiral staircase to check things out and I heard the band saw kick on, too.

"Now I was even more upset," Bill explained, "because it sounded as if someone were just playing around in the shop. Next the drill press came on and then the radial arm saw— that was the final straw! But the odd thing was that in spite of the fact that I heard all the saws running at once, I couldn't hear any wood being cut.

"From the top of the stairs I yelled for whoever was in the shop to get out, but I got no response. And just as I entered the shop door itself, all the saws suddenly shut off and everything was quiet again.

"There was no way that anyone could have turned off the saws and gotten out of the door that fast," Bill insisted. "In fact, the saws were all in different parts of the shop, so they couldn't even be turned off at the same time by just one person. And if anyone had run out, he would have had to pass right in front of me.

"Once again, I left the theater in a hurry—without locking up or even turning off the lights in the makeup room. I called the department head to tell him what I had done, and he told me that he understood completely because the same thing had happened to him."

The unexplained phenomena at the MSU theater seemed to intensify the next weekend with the opening of "Damn Yankees," a play in which the protagonist sells his soul to the devil to become a baseball star. Half an hour before curtain, a huge paint rack that had been suspended from cables broke loose and crashed down onto the floor of the shop. Even though the area was full of people, the only person to hear the rack fall was the set director, who was also playing the part of the devil.

"The cable looked as if it had been sliced cleanly in two," Bill remembered. "If it had broken after wearing down, or even if someone had sawed it, it would have had a few frayed ends. But the smoothness of the cut was a total mystery."

Throughout the first act, more unsettling events plagued

the cast and crew. First, a woman was frightened to see a noose hanging off the catwalk when it definitely had not been there five minutes earlier. Then the actors on stage clearly heard the explosion of a lighting instrument, but no shattered glass was ever found. And finally, the set director playing the devil tumbled from some steps into the first row of the audience, later claiming that he'd felt someone pulling the stairs right out from under him.

The spooky events weren't limited to the stage area, however. While the first act was still going on, Bill Koch took a break and went to the men's restroom. "As I was standing in there, I plainly heard a low unearthly laugh coming from the area right above my head, in the truss system only a foot under the ceiling," he said. "I ran out as soon as I could, and just as I reached the metal staircase a power surge in the stairwell made the lights pulsate weirdly. The area was so hot that it felt like a fire was burning, and when I got back to the stage I was so scared I could barely catch my breath.

"But for some reason, after intermission everything ran smoothly," Bill said. "I realized, though, that I'd definitely had my share of 'Jon Schmidt' experiences."

Bill was to have one more, however, when he heard the eerie laugh again several months later. He and two friends were sitting in the makeup room telling stories about the psychic phenomena at the theater. "Suddenly, that same hideous laugh came from the washroom below us," Bill said. "We immediately went to investigate, but no one was there. I was relieved, though, that someone besides me had finally heard it."

Bill continued to appear in productions after his graduation in 1985, and he recalls one evening when he had a feeling of impending danger while helping to hang lights. "I told the guy working with me that I thought something was going to happen, and that he should stay away from the electrical equipment for a while. And, sure enough, the light board shorted out. If he had continued working he would have been shocked."

That same night Bill was standing backstage in an old light booth, and he and the person next to him witnessed a free-floating transparent apparition that looked like a woman's skirt. The white wavy thing wafted through the air for a minute or so, then sped up to go between the watchers, forcing them out of the way before it disappeared. "I experienced the oddest sensation of hot and cold at the same time," Bill said, "and I have no idea what we saw.

"I didn't have any other unusual experiences at MSU, but one interesting coincidence did occur," Bill added. "I was working on my senior project at my home theater, the Blue Slipper in Livingston. The building was being remodeled, and a vinyl upholstery material had been put on the walls to cover them. There was a seam in the material, behind which people had stuck business cards. I peeled back the little lip of vinyl and pulled out the first one I found. Guess whose it was? Jon Schmidt's!"

Bill recalls one other experience linking him to the former theater director. At the time Schmidt died, there had been some wild talk and unsubstantiated speculation that someone had purposely caused his accident. The rumor was that some kind of oil used by the military might have been poured on the stairwell to make it even more slippery. "No one had ever been able to prove that oil had been poured on the stairs, and no container for it was ever found," Bill said. "But once when I was cleaning out the tool room, I found a bottle of this oil behind a built-in rack."

While practically no one now believes that Schmidt's fall was anything more than a tragic accident, almost everyone I talked to in the theater department has claimed to feel a presence, either Schmidt's on that of the unidentified woman phantom. Current director Joel Jahnkt admits that he left the building one night after sensing that he was not alone, and two sound engineers almost walked out for the same reason claiming that they had a bad case of "the willies."

If that's what they had, an epidemic of "the willies" must be making the rounds of the MSU drama department, where what goes on behind the scenes is just as dramatic as the performances themselves.

THE LONELY LADY AND OTHER GHOSTS
OF CHICO HOT SPRINGS

The Chico Hot Springs Lodge and Ranch in Montana's aptly named Paradise Valley is famous for its steaming thermal pools and its superb gourmet cuisine; but in recent years, it has become almost as well known for its psychic phenomena.

It isn't surprising that Chico has such star-quality spooks, not when you consider that the combination restaurant, hotel, and resort is also a favorite "haunt" of celebrities such as Peter Fonda, Jeff Bridges, and Dennis Quaid. In the old days, Chico even hosted famed cowboy artist Charles Russell, who traded drawings on the back of stationery for drinks, and President Theodore Roosevelt, who stayed there the night before he visited Yellowstone National Park, thirty miles to the south.

Originally named the Chico Warm Springs Hotel, the establishment opened to the public on June 20, 1900. Owners Bill and Percie Matheson Knowles enjoyed the resort as much as any of their guests, although Percie did have strong qualms about drinking. Over her objections, Bill constructed a saloon and dance hall on the property, and the resort became even more successful, promoting itself as a place to cure "rheumatism, stomach and kidney troubles, and all skin and blood diseases."

Perhaps Bill Knowles should have spent more time in the hot pools and less in the saloon, because on April 22, 1910, he died of cirrhosis of the liver. He was buried a few days later at nearby Chico Cemetery, leaving Percie and the couple's twelve-year-old son, Radbourne, to run the business.

Percie's dream was to turn the retreat into a real healthcare center, and her first action was to close the saloon she detested. In 1912, she persuaded Dr. George A. Townsend to make the hotel his headquarters, and he was so successful in treating patients that Chico's fame spread quickly to surrounding states. Over the next five years the pools were enlarged, and a hospital wing was added.

Dr. Townsend stayed at Chico Hot Springs for thirteen years, but finally the hard work became too much for him. He retired in 1925, and even though other doctors came to take his place, the resort would never again enjoy a fine reputation as a hospital.

Radbourne Knowles moved away to get married, and Chico attracted fewer patients every year. As Percie's beloved resort began to decline, so did she. Her mind as well as her body gave way to the pressures of running a failing business, and for a long time she was confined to her room in the hotel. In 1936 she was admitted to the state hospital in Warm Springs, where she died four and a half years later.

After Radbourne's death in 1943, Chico Hot Springs went through a series of owners who couldn't decide whether to make it a health resort, a vacation getaway, or a combination of both. In 1973, Mike and Eve Art bought the property, and three years later they moved from Cleveland, Ohio, to live on it. Since then they've made many improvements, so that once again Bill and Percie's resort is thriving.

And so is the ghostly activity at the old lodge. Could the Arts' refurbishment of Chico have caused the burst of psychic phenomena reported by guests and employees alike? This might be possible, except that former owner John Sterhan recalls that during his tenure, from 1967 to 1972, the staff also reported strange events. The most common belief among those who have had eerie encounters at Chico is that the Knowleses, especially Percie, have never left.

Earl Murray wrote about the otherworldly occupants of the resort in his "Ghosts of the Old West" (Chicago: Contemporary Books, 1988). In "The Hot Springs Phantom," he describes the weird experience of two security officers, Tim Barnes and Ron Woolery, around 2:20 A.M. one Sunday in May 1986. The two guards had waited for all the customers and employees of the Chico Saloon to leave, then they locked the doors and returned to the hotel via the board walkway. At this time, Tim had been working for the resort for eight years, and he'd never believed his coworkers' spooky stories. Just as he opened the door leading into the lobby, he saw something and suddenly froze.

"Look," Tim said, and pointed across the room in the direction of an old piano.

The two security officers stared in amazement at the sight before them. A white filmy figure hovered just above the floor near the piano, and the smoky features of a face stared back at them. Only the head and upper body were distinct; the rest of the apparition was a formless mass trailing away to nothing.

"It was an eerie feeling, the kind that makes the hair stand up on the back of your neck," Tim said, when I interviewed him in October 1991. "I wasn't afraid of it, but I realized that we were definitely looking at something supernatural. We kept staring at the ghost, and I finally got the idea to take a picture of it with a Polaroid camera in the office."

To get to the office required courage, because it meant walking close to the figure. Tim steeled himself and hurried around the phantom and through the door. He found the camera, but because it didn't belong to him and because he was nervous, he couldn't figure out how to attach the flash bar.

"I decided to take the picture without the flash, and the results weren't very good," he said. "There's one tiny white unidentifiable spot in the middle of the photograph. Whatever we saw was definitely in the basic form of a person, but we couldn't tell what sex it was. It must have hovered by the piano for a good two minutes, but after I took the picture the hazy form just dispersed like smoke."

Tim is now the general manager of Chico Hot Springs, and he's joined the ranks of those who are certain that the old hotel is haunted. His mother, Edie Mundell, is another person who knows from firsthand experience that the phantom is real. She worked as a night auditor there for three years and had just quit her job when I talked to her, also in October 1991. Edie's encounter was very similar to that of her son.

"I've been interested in metaphysical subjects for a long time, so I thought I'd be well prepared if I ever saw the ghost," she explained. "On the morning when I finally did, everything had been very quiet. I needed to get a printout on the credit card machine, and I walked into the dining room to pick it up. At the same time, the security guard who had just finished his rounds was coming through the front door along with some people working the breakfast shift. I heard them all talking together.

"The dining room was dark because I hadn't turned the lights on, Edie continued, "and for some reason, I suddenly had an impulse to look behind me, through the back of the dining room and into the small lounge. And there, standing at the door to the lounge, was an apparition.

"It was cloudy and all white, just like ghosts are often portrayed in the movies. It was smoky and hazy, but it was shaped like a person. I think it was a woman, but I'm not sure. Looking at it gave me the weirdest feeling, and even though I thought I would be well prepared for such an encounter, I wasn't. I think I startled that ghost nearly as much it startled me—I could sense fear coming from both of us. I don't think the spirit noticed me until I began walking quickly away from it. I got out of there before it had time to disappear."

Around the time of my interview with Edie Mundell, bartender Terrie Angell encountered the same apparition in another part of the darkened dining room at about three o'clock one morning. "Even now I can't tell you whether or not I believe in ghosts," she told me, "but I could definitely feel her presence as soon as I walked through the door. And there she was, sitting in a chair on the left-hand side of the room. Because it was dark, I can't describe what she looked like except to say that the image seemed more hazy than solid. I ran out of that dining room as fast as I could; even talking about it now gives me goose bumps."

Fellow employee Lindy Moore was equally terrified by her encounter with the filmy phantom in the winter of 1989. "I had gone up to the second floor to put a blanket in a room, and all of a sudden I became aware that someone else was there," she said. "I turned around and saw the apparition very clearly. I'm sure it was Percie. She was wearing a dress and she appeared to be floating. The figure was cloudy and misty, but I could definitely see her features. She had a fairly blank expression on her face, but I'm sure she could see me.

"I'd never actually seen a ghost before, and it scared the heck out of me," Lindy admitted. "I stood there for probably twenty seconds, and part of me really wanted to stay to find out what would happen next. But when the form started to move toward me, I changed my mind in a hurry and got out of there. Thinking back over the experience now, I believe something very interesting would have happened if I had stayed in the room, but I was just too scared. And I've never seen her since."

Former security guard Larry Bohne has probably gotten a closer look at Chico's lady spook than has anyone else. Larry hastens to explain that he is by nature a highly logical and analytical person, having worked as an air traffic controller for the U.S. Air Force, and as a soils and concrete lab inspector for the U.S. Army Corps of Engineers. His other work, as an ambulance technician and a volunteer firefighter, also required equal measures of cool observation and common sense. Larry had been employed at Chico Hot Springs for about fifteen months when he had one of the eeriest encounters ever reported there.

"It was the third week of January 1990, and I was used to being alone in the old hotel," he said. "During the winter months it usually has only a few guests at any one time, and on this night they were in rooms on the main floor just off the lobby. Besides them and me, the only other person in the hotel was the night auditor in the main office.

"Even though no one was staying on the second and third floors, it was still my job to make routine fire checks in these areas," Larry said. "One one of my rounds, at about 2:30 A.M., I was walking along the second floor hallway, and as I passed the stairwell leading to the third floor I could sense that someone was at the head of the stairs. I stepped back a few paces to the bottom of the stairwell and looked up to see a matronly lady standing at the top landing looking down at me.

"That seemed unusual because I was sure there were no registered guests above the first floor," Larry explained. "The lady appeared to be about five feet four to five feet six inches tall and approximately forty-five to fifty years old. Her face, though clearly defined, seemed pale and without expression. It was obvious that she was looking at me, but she didn't acknowledge my presence in any way. She wore a full-length pale blue dress with a high collar and long sleeves and the material was printed with what looked like tiny white flowers. Her graying hair was in a tight bun, and her hands were clasped in front of her.

"Thinking that she was a guest who had gotten lost, I asked if I could help her. When I spoke, she silently turned away and moved into the darkness of the third floor hallway behind her. I say 'moved,' because she didn't seem to be walking—she just drifted away without any movement of her upper torso. I couldn't even detect any leg movement under the long dress.

"I went up to the main hallway of the third floor, but I could see nothing," Larry said. "Everything was dark except for some soft light from the courtyard below that filtered into the window at the end of the hall. The lady I had seen so clearly just seconds before had vanished.

"All the rooms on that floor are kept locked, so I guessed that the only place she could have gone would have been into one of the bathrooms, which are not locked. As I walked down the hall, I detected a sweet fragrance in the vicinity of rooms 346 through 350. I checked the bathrooms, but they were empty and dark. I retraced my steps down the hallway and again smelled the sweet scent in the same area as before. It reminded me of jasmine or lilac, and it was strongest near room 349. "I used my security passkey to unlock the door. The room was silent and dark, and I shone my flashlight inside. Then I noticed that the rocking chair in the corner by the window was gently moving back and forth. I quickly flipped the light switch on, and I saw the chair stop rocking instantly, as if someone invisible had been sitting in it and made it stop. I checked the window and noted that it was tightly shut. But even if it had been open, the night was extremely calm, without any wind to make the chair rock. And if the movement had been caused by wind, the chair would not have stopped rocking so suddenly. I also realized that the sweet fragrance that had been so strong before had now completely faded away.

"The entire episode lasted about five or six minutes," Larry said, "and afterward I was eager to return to the reality of the main office and the reassuring company of Edie Mundell, the night auditor. I was so unnerved that it took me several cups of coffee to muster up the nerve to tell her what had happened; when I did, she smiled and said, 'Welcome to the Percie Club.'

"Edie also told me that room 349 was the one in which Percie Knowles had lived during her last days at Chico," Larry explained. "She had become quite senile and spent nearly all her waking hours in a rocking chair, staring out the window at Emigrant Peak behind the hotel."

Security guard Charlie Wells had an experience similar to Larry's when he worked part-time at Chico in 1989 and 1990. But while Larry initially believed that the woman he saw was flesh and blood, Charlie was made immediately aware that the lady ascending the stairs from the second to the third floor was not of this world.

"I came up out of the lobby on one of my rounds, and all I saw at first was a kind of mist," Charlie explained. "I could see features, but it seemed as if I were seeing her through a smoke-filled room. I saw her arms, but no hands and no legs, and I could just make out a face. She appeared to be floating rather than walking up the stairs, and she was wearing a long, flowing white dress. In fact, it looked a lot like the one that Percie Knowles is wearing in a picture hanging in the lobby."

Charlie often had the disquieting experience of finding the door to Room 349 unlocked and open. "This was during the wintertime when business was slow," he said. "I knew the room hadn't been rented out, so I'd lock it up; but the door would be open again when I made my next round. I was the only one there before the auditor arrived, and I was the only one with the keys. The other keys were all locked away.

"Another time, I was locking the outside door to the saloon when I noticed a light on in the lounge," he continued. "A man and a woman were sitting at a table near the window in the dining room off to the right. I couldn't make out many details, but I did see that the woman was wearing a long white dress. I knew that the cooks, the waitresses, and the dishwashers had all left after dinner, and I thought that maybe the owner's daughter, Andy Art, had come back with her boyfriend to have a drink.

"I went on into the lobby, and I could tell that the night auditor hadn't arrived yet," Charlie said. "Then I walked over to the dining room doors, opened them, and saw that no one was in there. But two chairs were pulled out, and there were two glasses on a table. The next night I questioned the cocktail waitress, and she insisted that she had cleaned everything up and left the room in order. I'll always wonder whether the two figures I saw were Bill and Percie Knowles."

Charlie also found unexpected disarray in the kitchen one night after all the staff had gone home. On his first round everything was in order, but the next time he checked the area he found knives, dishes, and a variety of other utensils scattered across the cooks' table.

More than a few employees of Chico Hot Springs have reported hearing the clattering and crashing of pots and pans from the kitchen when they knew no one was there. About three weeks after he followed the ghost of Percie into room 349, Larry Bohne was tending the lobby fireplace at 3:00 A.M. and wishing he had someone to talk with.

"There were no guests in the hotel, so I was the only person on the premises," he recalled. "Even the night auditor wasn't due in for another hour and a half. But suddenly, from the kitchen area, I heard the clanging and rattling of dishes and pots and pans, as if someone were busily cooking or cleaning up.

"I knew I was supposed to be alone, so I went to investigate," Larry said. "But just as I approached the kitchen from the dining room the sounds stopped, as if someone had suddenly switched them off. I entered the kitchen, which was still dark, and when I turned on the lights, every thing appeared to be in its place—nothing was out of the ordinary in any way. Immediately, I checked the exit to the outside courtyard and the door to housekeeping. Both were just as I had found them on earlier rounds, tightly secured. The only other way to enter the kitchen was from the dining room door through which I had gone myself.

"As I left the kitchen, I turned off the lights. At the same time, the telephone began to ring. Rather than go all the way back to the office I switched on the lights again and answered the phone in the kitchen But instead of hearing a voice on the other end of the line, I heard what I can only describe as an electrical hum, totally different from the sound of a dial tone. I hung up the phone and then picked it up to listen. This time I heard only a normal dial tone.

"I turned off the lights once again and started walking back to the office," Larry continued. "I had gotten as far as the dining room when loud music started blaring out of the kitchen.

"This time I just knew that a trickster was at work, so I sneaked back again and shone my flashlight into the room. It was completely empty, but I noticed that the music was coming from the employees' radio—though the power switch was in the off position!

"I flipped the switch on and off several times, but I couldn't get the music to stop or the volume to decrease," Larry explained. "The noise stopped only when I pulled the plug from the socket. And when I plugged the cord back in to test the radio, everything worked normally.

"Maybe what happened with the telephone and the radio could be attributed to some kind of electrical glitch," he admitted, "but this episode left me very unsettled. And I've never been able to explain away the sound of the clattering dishes when, obviously, no one was present."

During this same winter, Larry's twenty-year-old son Mike also became a security guard at Chico Hot Springs, and his initiation into "the Percie Club" was just as uncanny as his father's had been. "If Mike said something happened to him, it did," Larry insisted. "He's not one to let his imagination run wild, and the jobs he's had couldn't be done by a person who panics easily. At sixteen, for example, he was the youngest state-certified ambulance technician ever in Montana, and he's also served with search and rescue units, earning the rank of major with the U.S. Air Force Civil Air Patrol. It's also interesting to note that Mike had never heard about my experiences with Percie until after he had tangled with her himself."

Before the young man's first night of duty in the hotel, his senior partner gave him a copy of Earl Murray's "Ghosts of the Old West." But even levelheaded Mike doubted the wisdom of reading the chapter about the Hot Springs phantom while he was alone on his first evening watch.

"But, naturally, common sense soon gave way to curiosity," Mike admitted, "so I went ahead and read it, and for the rest of that night all the creaks, cracks, and other noises kept my nerves on edge. But I didn't actually encounter Percie Knowles' ghost itself until I'd been working there three weeks, just long enough so that I no longer grew apprehensive at every little sound.

"At about three o'clock on one bitterly cold January morning, I was stoking the main fire and completing some paperwork after having made several rounds of the complex," he said. "Only one room on the main floor of the hotel was occupied; a few more had been rented out to guests in the lower lodge about three hundred yards from the main building. The night auditor had not yet arrived.

"I took a break and made my way through the dining room toward the restrooms in the rear," Mike continued. "As I approached the small lounge at the end of the dining room, I noticed that the tables and chairs were arranged so that there was a clear straight aisle to the restrooms. This seemed a little odd because the furniture was usually set up in such a way that you had to take a twisted path around it to get to the bathrooms.

"I also noticed that the dining room and lounge area felt unusually cold as I walked through it, and it felt just as chilly when I returned from the restroom. It's highly unusual for the area near the kitchen to be any thing but cozy and warm because it usually retains the heat from the day's cooking. It also struck me as odd that several chairs were now blocking the clear path I had taken on the way into the men's room I actually had to move them before I could get through the area am return to my office. I thought that the night auditor must have arrived early and moved the chairs for some reason.

"When I got back to the office I expected to see her, but no one was there," Mike said. "An uneasy feeling crept up my spine. To settle my nerves, I decided to take a walk around the outside of the main lodge and as I strolled past the parking space reserved for the night auditor I saw that it was still empty.

"The air was so cold that my nose felt numb so I went back to the hotel lobby. I stoked the fire and returned to my paperwork. Soon afterward, Edie (the night auditor) arrived, booted up the computers, an went back to the kitchen to fix herself a cup of coffee. When she returned she commented on the unusual chill coming from the kitchen, and both attributed it to the fact that it was so cold outside.

"Edie and I were engrossed in our paperwork when we were sudden interrupted by the sounds of dishes clinking," Mike said. "We looked and joked that Percie must be busy at work because the kitchen cook wasn't expected for another hour. The noises continued for so long the curiosity got the best of me. As I made my way back to the kitchen it seemed peculiar that even though I was approaching nearer to the clanking, it didn't sound any louder to me. When I was about twenty feet from the kitchen, the dish-rattling stopped completely.

"I entered the kitchen and was immediately hit with a blast of air so cold that it vaporized my breath," Mike said. "There was not much light, but as I peered across the room I could plainly see a woman with her back to me. Time seemed to come to a stop, and I felt an eerie sense of calm.

"The woman gave no sign that she noticed me," Mike continued. "She remained standing still without changing position, and I noticed that her hair was piled on top of her head. She was wearing a long dress and, as I continued to stare at her, I noticed that her hem was about six inches from the ground and nothing was visible between it and the floor.

"I felt dizzy. I was afraid to stay but more afraid to move, so I stood frozen just inside the kitchen door. Suddenly, for no apparent reason, the woman moved forward with a motion that was unlike walking. She went out a door, and I know I saw it close behind her; she was gone and the chill that had been in the room dispersed instantly.

"The door she exited from is padlocked from the outside, and there is no way to unlock it from the inside," Mike explained. "I had checked that door several times on my rounds that evening, and I knew that I had the only key to the lock except for the one that general manager Tim Barnes always keeps with him. On that night, Tim and the other set of keys were two hundred miles away in Billings, where he was attending a conference. I checked again to see if I could open the door from inside the kitchen, but it wouldn't budge."

In addition to seeing Percie's apparition and hearing her bang pots and pans around in a very chilly kitchen, the employees of Chico Hot Springs also report a variety of other phenomena apparently related to her. Security guard Charlie Wells was in the lobby one night when he heard the mysterious sound of a woman moaning. He looked for the source of the noise for at least forty-five minutes but was never able to track it down. Housekeepers hear doors slamming on the third floor when they know they're supposed to be alone on that level, and they often feel an unseen presence in the rooms there. And no matter where they place the chair that Larry Bohne saw rocking in room 349, it reputedly always returns to a certain spot facing the window. A bible in the attic is said to remain mysteriously free of dust and is always open to the same page in the Psalms, even after employees have purposely left it open elsewhere. At different times, a feather and a handkerchief have been placed on the open pages, and those who checked later found no trace of the feather and no footprints on the floor of the dusty attic. The handkerchief was found later in the saloon.

The Arts' daughter Andy believes in the ghost, but she distrusts the legend about the bible because so many people now have access to the keys to the attic. But no one has been able to explain a tray of candles that apparently lighted themselves in the kitchen, or a single candle that was found burning again after Charlie Wells knew he had extinguished it.

Charlie says that even animals occasionally sense something awry at Chico. He recalls the time that a "Heinz 57" breed of dog was so afraid to walk down a hallway that he fell, shaking with fear and wetting the carpet, when his owner demanded that he come to him.

"The Knowleses are supposedly buried just up the road from the hotel," Charlie explained, laughing. "And the security guard who helped break me in said that there's a big gopher hole in Percie's grave and that how she got out."

In addition to giving the employees of the lodge an occasional scare Percie apparently enjoys playing tricks on them, too. Her specialty is making things disappear—especially when they're needed the most.

"In the summer of 1991 we lost a rooming list for a group that was coming in," explained Lindy Moore. "We were all working with it out on the front desk and all of a sudden it was gone. We turned this place upside down looking for it, but we never found it. The group came and went and about a week after they had gone I walked into the office and the list we'd been searching for was lying right out on the desk.

"On another occasion, I was the only person in the room and I set down a file to answer the phone," she continued. "When I tried to find the file again it was nowhere to be seen. But when I was getting ready to drive back home after work that day, guess what I found on the seat of my car? The file looked just as if it were supposed to be there. Things are always disappearing and reappearing in very strange places."

Percie has pulled so many pranks on the hotel staff that Edie Mundell thinks her spirit might have regressed to the time when she was twelve years old. 'When I saw the ghost, I had the feeling that she was a you girl," the night auditor explained. "Maybe Percie was happiest at the time of her life and that's why I perceived her as being so young. And she certainly acts like a kid."

Edie explained that Percie is especially attracted to coins. "Once I was counting my money and I came up a nickel short," she said. "I searched for it for quite a while and then I gave up because it just wasn't there.

A couple of hours later, when I'd forgotten all about it, I

found the nickel way out on the front counter. I hadn't been anywhere near that area, and I can't imagine why anyone would leave a lone nickel there."

On another occasion, Edie dropped a coin on the floor, saw where it landed, but decided to wait until she finished counting to pick it up. When she finally reached down to retrieve it, it was no longer there. Instead, it had traveled to the table where security guard Charlie Wells made out his evening reports. Charlie vouches for Edie's story and swears that he didn't take the coin himself.

Most of the strange incidents at Chico are believed to be caused by Percie and most of the apparitions seem to be of her. But several employees have seen what they thought were male ghosts or at least spooks of undetermined gender. Many of these sightings have occurred in the area above the bar called the annex, where many employees live. Maintenance man Bob Oppelt was living in the annex in the winter of 1989, and his story is one of the most frightening of all.

"I had gone to bed and was just about to fall asleep," he recalled. "It was fairly dark but a little light from outside was coming in through the window. Suddenly, a tall figure appeared in the corner of my room. It hovered off of the ground, extending almost to the ceiling.

"I couldn't believe what I was seeing, so I closed my eyes, thinking whatever it was would go away," Bob said. "But when I opened them and dared to look again, the awful thing was still there, hovering just below the high ceiling of the room. And, even worse, it began moving, waving away from the wall and down toward me, then back again. No individual parts of its body moved; it just moved all together in this peculiar waving motion.

"I couldn't see too clearly, but the figure looked like that of a very tall man wearing something like an overcoat," Bob explained. "I could make out the definite outline of a beard and the facial features, too. My hair was standing on end and I'll never forget the eerie feeling in the air, almost like electricity. The apparition didn't reach out for me but it kept waving down toward me. Finally, after four or five motions away from the wall and back again, the ghost came right down next to me as I lay in bed.

"I tried to scream, but my throat was paralyzed," Bob said. "I remember rolling out of bed and crawling out into the hallway on my hands and knees. For quite a while I couldn't bear to go back into my room; after I finally did, I lay in bed with the light on for a long time.

"At first I didn't tell anybody about what had happened because I was afraid people would think I was crazy. I told my story only after I found out that my brother had had a similar experience two weeks later in his room at the other end of the hall.

"His girlfriend had just come out of his room and he was lying the bed with the light out saying his prayers," Bob said. "Suddenly felt something pressing on his chest, and then whatever it was still shaking him. His bed was right against the wall, making it difficult for him to get away. Then this thing started bouncing him off the wall so loudly that the guy living in the room next door could hear it. Eventually the presence went away and left my brother alone.

"I don't know if the form I saw in my room was the same thing that visited my brother," Bob said. "But I know that neither my brother, nor I will ever forget what happened to us."

Andy Art was living in a small cabin across the road from the hotel when she, too, experienced an unwelcome nocturnal visitor. "I usually sleep on my side," she began, "and one night I felt something tap me on the waist. I remember flipping over, startled, and feeling that someone was in the room with me. Then I saw a hazy shape nearby. The head and shoulders were very distinct, but the rest of the body seemed to be flowing like a shapeless nightgown.

"I lay there looking at the thing beside my bed. It didn't move; it stayed in place and I sensed that it was looking at me, although I couldn't make out eyes or any other facial features," Andy recalled. "I sat up and wondered if I were still dreaming. I tried to adjust my eyes, thinking the form would disappear, but it was still there. It must have remained in room for about ten minutes. I was terrified, but I didn't know what to do, so I just sat on the edge of my bed and looked at it. It didn't threaten me any way and eventually it just floated away and faded from view.

"This happened in the late seventies, when I was about seventy Andy said. "I've always considered myself to be somewhat psychic because I often know who's calling me before I answer the phone. But that was the first time I had ever seen a ghost."

Another encounter with a vague hazy entity occurred when Andy was living on the third floor of the hotel. "I was staying at the far end, opposite the attic entrance," she explained, "and I remember getting up one night to go to the bathroom. I was walking down the hall when I looked up to see this same kind of misty cloudy form. Again, the shape of the head and shoulders was fairly distinct and everything below it just seemed to flow away to nothing. The figure was walking toward me and I was very startled. But this time it moved away and disappeared without coming close to me. I don't know if it went into a wall or what, but suddenly it wasn't there any longer. I remember having a hard time getting back to sleep after that."

Andy believes that many manifestations may be attributable to the fact that the hotel was a hospital for so many years. "I'm sure that a lot of people have come in and out of the world at Chico Hot Springs, so many spirits may reside here," she said. "I've seen phantoms two or three times in the lounge behind the dining room, and that area was at one time part of the hospital. One night, my boyfriend was in the bathroom and I was in the kitchen and, simultaneously, we both felt a presence with us. At first we each thought the other had come in to play a trick, but then we realized that that wasn't true."

Andy believes that the spirits may also be attracted to the furniture in the dining room. "There's a good chance that some of it may actually have belonged to Bill and Percie Knowles," she explained. "Lots of it dates back at least to the 1920s or 1930s, and most of the owners previous to my parents didn't put much money into new pieces, at least as far as I know."

Andy also wonders if an odd discovery made behind the hotel has anything to do with the psychic phenomena. When the Arts moved to Chico Hot Springs, they had to dig a new septic line. "Way down deep we found some very strange things," Andy said. "There were gold fillings with a piece of tooth still attached, a pair of men's beat-up shoes, and, as I recall, some eyeglasses. It made you wonder if someone had died down there, except that there were no bones or other clothing. There are many strange stories at Chico about a Chinese gardener who disappeared. Who knows if these were his things or someone else's? Finding these long-buried objects gave us a very strange feeling, almost as if we didn't want to disturb them. We felt somehow that they were supposed to be there."

Regardless of who, besides Percie Knowles, the other ghostly inhabitants of Chico might be, the employees agree that the paranormal activities are most common in winter and often in the dead of night, when everything is quiet and the hotel is much less busy. It is probably also significant that so many of the stories involve an intense feeling of cold and only partial materialization of spirits—from hazy indistinct figures with no discernible features to those who are so solidly formed that they look like flesh-and-blood creatures, except that they might be missing hands, or feet, or everything below the knees.

Both the coldness and the misty incomplete formation of specters may be understood more easily if we think of ghosts as manifestations of energy. The chill that so often accompanies the sighting of apparitions or other kinds of psychic phenomena may be explained by the theory that when spirits return to the earthly plane of existence they require a lot of energy to make themselves seen or heard. They may draw some of this energy from the physical environment. Heat is a form of energy so when the ghost takes energy from its surroundings the air is apt to feel cold. As soon as the spook vanishes, however, so does the chill. Likewise, the hazy or partial materialization of spirits might be more easily understood if we liken ghosts to television signals, which are broadcast through the air to be picked up by receivers. Under conditions and circumstances not yet understood, ghosts, like TV signals, may sometimes "come in" loud and clear, while at other times their "reception" is faulty or incomplete. At these times, we might not see them at all, or they may appear misty, transparent, or even lacking crucial body parts. But if we accept the idea that any kind of manifestation requires tremendous amounts of energy, we shouldn't be surprised to find that sometimes our ghosts just aren't "all there."

Sometimes, in fact, a ghost may not look like a person at all. According to Earl Murray's "Ghosts of the Old West," a group of teenagers and young adults were having a New Year's Eve party at Chico, and they were jumping from a roof into the hot pool. Suddenly a mysterious white light began moving along the roofline. The party-goers interpreted the light as a warning that they should get down; indeed, serious accidents had occurred previously when young people played on the roof.

There's no guarantee, of course, that anyone visiting Chico Hot Springs Lodge and Ranch will have a paranormal experience—ghosts may abound at this lovely resort, but they don't perform on demand. In fact, guests at Chico are usually so busy enjoying the pleasures of this world—scrumptious food, relaxing hot pools, and towering snowcapped peaks— that they have little time left to think about the next one. But if you really want to have an unearthly encounter, come to Chico Hot Springs in the dead of winter and stroll on the third floor of the hotel around three o'clock in the morning. If you catch a whiff of lilac or jasmine near room 349, put your ear to the door and listen. You might hear the sounds of the rocking chair swaying back and forth, back and forth, as a lonely lady stares from her window into the blackness of night.

ABOUT THE AUTHOR

Debra Munn, a native of Amarillo, Texas, is a descendant of miners who lived in Butte and Anaconda, Montana, at the beginning of the twentieth century. In 1995 she moved to Brighton, East Sussex, in England, where she lives with her husband, Mick Henry. Debra has a Ph.D. in American literature from Florida State University and has published short stories, essays and articles on a variety of subjects. Her *Sussex Haunted Heritage: Historic Properties Open to the Public* was published in England in 2006 by S.B. Publications; and *Ghosts on the Range: Eerie True Tales of Wyoming* was published in 1989 by Pruett Publishing of Boulder, Colorado. Debra is also the creator and marketer of *coupleconnect* relationship enhancement cards.

Here's another spooky book...

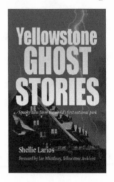

YELLOWSTONE GHOST STORIES
By Shellie Larios
Yellowstone National Park is haunted—or is it? You'll think so after reading the tales in this book. The stories include a little lost boy who appears and disappears among crowds of tourists, a headless bride at Old Faithful Inn, and numerous ghostly spirits, mysterious sounds, and strange apparitions. This is a great book to read late at night around your campfire—if you dare.

A few more Montana books by Riverbend Publishing...

MONTANA TRIVIA
By Janet Spencer
Q: Where are the answers to 1,263 questions about Montana?
A: Here!
This book is your personal compendium of the most incredible, unbelievable, wild, weird, arcane, fun, fascinating, and true facts about Montana. Great easy reading. Fun games at the end of every section!

COPPER CAMP: THE LUSTY STORY OF BUTTE, MONTANA
Writers Project of Montana
The classic Montana book that tells it all! From the miners to the kids to the girls of the line, *Copper Camp* is the people's story of the Richest Hill on Earth during its wild and wide-open heyday. "A fascinating, raw-boned read! Excellent." *Great Falls Tribune*

THE MAN WHO SHOT LIBERTY VALANCE
By Dorothy M. Johnson
The Western Writer's of America ranked these four stories by Montana's Johnson as the best short stories of the 20th Century. In addition to the title story, the book includes "The Hanging Tree," "A Man Called Horse," and "Lost Sister."

www.riverbendpublishing.com